POCKETKNIFE KITTY

SHANNON RILEY

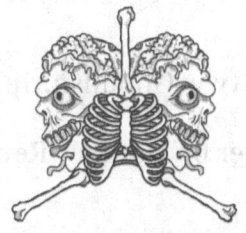

Ghoulish Books
San Antonio, Texas

Pocketknife Kitty
Copyright © 2024 Shannon Riley

First Edition

ISBN: 978-1-963801-00-2

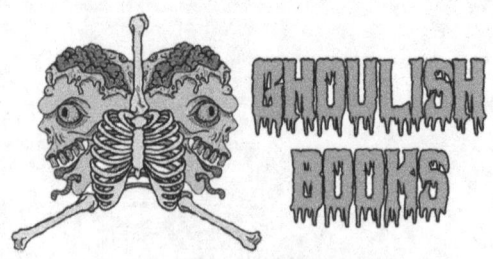

www.Ghoulish.rip

Cover by Matthew Revert

To the women who know to choose the bear.

1.

From: Price, Carrie <carrie_the_one@firstmail.com>
To: Doe, Julie <anon821425@firstmail.com>
Sent: 30 March 2022, 11:12 a.m.
Subject: Re: Information- DON'T DELETE

Who is this?

Carrie
Sent from my iPhone

FOR THE MOST PART, it was just like any other bar. Musty, loud, and full of dead people.

Jamie sat in BAR NEON; a newish creation brought to town by a pair of wealthy "entrepreneurs" doing their best to revitalize an otherwise dying former steel town. The duo had been the subject of a moderate amount of buzz at work since they came in to apply for a handful of business loans a few weeks back. A few of the younger girls were practically frenzied at the prospect of a new place to gather, to drink, to dance, but Jamie remained neutral. Cautious, even. She'd seen this before. Every few years, some investment group or generally well-meaning new money capitalist would do their best to rescue the town, and staunch the flow of twenty-somethings making their mass exoduses to the next big city. Millennials wanted fast casual dining. They wanted coffee shops. This town had neither.

What else this town didn't have was money, and soon those hopeful investors would close up shop and also move out alongside the most recent migration.

Those left behind were a common breed.

Many of them, Jamie recalled, stayed because they impregnated their girlfriend in high school and couldn't leave without the threat that they'd never see their kid again. Some remained in duty as the sole caregivers to elderly parents, grandparents, or disabled siblings. But usually they stayed because they didn't know what else to do. If they were lucky, they got out from under their parents by the time they graduated college, if they went, and roomed with someone they knew in high school. But big moves are expensive and unpredictable. Starting over, meeting new people, choosing a new dentist, learning the gas stations with the best prices—it's hard. So they stay. They stay, they take care of their aging parents, they eventually move back in, have the next generation's children, take over ownership of their childhood home, bury the parents, and the cycle repeats.

One thing they had in common were their eyes. When they sat in a bar or a club, laughing with acquaintances and taking shots with friends, their eyes remained passive, unfocused. They weren't eyes that belonged to the living. They would scan the crowds, hopeful but resigned, like some ancient sadness. Their eyes tempered the emotions of the rest of their face, betraying them to what everyone else already knew. Jamie knew what they were thinking: *What have I done? Why am I here?* She knew their thoughts because those thoughts were also her own.

She wasn't entirely sure what compelled her to come out to the club. Maybe she was struck by curiosity, perhaps it was mostly boredom, maybe it was the vague hopefulness that maybe this time the local venture would be successful. The bartender made a decent margarita, Jamie had to admit, albeit a bit strong on the tequila. She took a cautious sip, nodding to the bartender as he made eye contact from the other end of the bar. Pretty good drink, even if the surrounding mood was lacking. As she patted her mouth with a napkin stamped with a contemporary looking "N," she scrolled through her phone, looking at nothing. She placed it down on the bar and surveyed the room.

She didn't recognize anybody. One would think such a thing was an anomaly in a small town, but as she got older, Jamie realized that was just the way of things. Every year produced another batch of fresh high school graduates, therefore pushing the strata of the older generations that much higher up, closer and closer to irrelevancy. Every time she came to a bar, she saw fewer peers. "Older" is of course relative; Jamie was only 30. Already 30? Some days it was difficult to distinguish how she felt about her age. *"I'm 27 years old. I've no money and no prospects. I'm already a burden to my parents,"* she thought to herself with a smile, hearing the voice of Charlotte Lucas, the outdated Pride and Prejudice meme ringing in her ears.

BAR NEON was larger on the inside than the modest exterior would lead one to believe. From her seat at the bar she had a good view of a large dance floor, although hardly anyone danced. Some undistinguishable pop music played loudly from the sound system; it sounded like a cover of something much older, but it was almost impossible to tell. Lining the walls of the club were small circular tables, many of which were empty. The lights were low, but the moving bodies were lit with an ethereal purple glow.

Her phone buzzed from its place on the bar. She tapped the screen, eyes momentarily adjusting from the sudden brightness. The text was short: *Where are you?* She chose to ignore it. Shortly following was another: *I want to talk can you come over?*

She turned the phone over and placed it back on the bar.

Jamie was suddenly aware of a presence directly to her right, a patron vying for the attention of the bartender. He smelled of crisp autumn air and tobacco, strong, as though he had only just come in from a smoke. The cold radiated off his coat, seeping into the flesh of Jamie's forearm. She wished she could press her flushed cheek against the leather of his sleeve. Jamie wasn't a smoker, but she loved the smell of tobacco. The earthiness, the warmth. She inhaled, eyed him in her periphery, and mumbled an unnecessary apology for being in the way. She leaned slightly left, giving him more room to signal for another drink.

It took her several seconds to realize he had spoken to her.

Jamie turned to face him. He seemed tall, but she was seated, so she couldn't be sure. He was fair with dark brown hair, and a pair of thick brows hooded two light eyes. He wasn't signaling the bartender at all. He looked at Jamie expectantly.

"I'm sorry, what was that?" Jamie said, a little louder than she meant. The music playing overhead made it harder to hear.

The man replied, "I asked if I could sit here."

On initial glance he was good looking. Not terribly attractive, but pleasant enough. His features were fair and anchored with a strong nose. However, the longer Jamie looked at him, the more disheveled he appeared. His beard was overgrown and a little wiry, stray hairs migrating down onto his throat. Beneath both eyes were dark shadows that could only have been caused by a lack of proper sleep, and his lips were chapped with dehydration. The gray t-shirt beneath his coat was wrinkled, and he wrung his hands together in . . . anxiety? Earnestness? Maybe he was just cold.

But he had a good smile about him, and she nodded.

He sat, sighed. "This place isn't too bad, is it?"

Jamie shrugged. "It's okay. This is the first time I've been out here."

"Me, too," he said. He combed his fingers through his

dark hair and smoothed his palm along his jawline. The back of his hand was prominent with veins, skin pale enough to reveal the blue spider webbing beneath. Jamie tried not to look. She sipped her margarita. "Some of the younger kids at work have been hyping this place up," he gave the dance floor a generous scan, "but for what, I don't know."

"Seems like we have the same coworkers," Jamie said.

"Bar *Neon*," he grinned, waving one of the bar napkins as he spoke. He rolled his eyes. Jamie offered him a mild smile. "Where do they think we are, Chicago? L.A.?"

"They'd be better off naming it Cow Tippers or something."

The man laughed. "Right, or The Double Wide."

"Or Free Dip Today Only," Jamie said, "That might actually draw a crowd."

He barked out another laugh. "Hey, that's pretty good. Don't be too loud or someone will nab that idea right from underneath you."

Jamie flourished a little bow gesture with a grin. She tipped her glass back, finishing the drink.

"What are you drinking?"

"Just a regular old margarita."

"Salt?"

She held up her glass, displaying a clean rim.

"Could you use another?"

Jamie smiled. She felt strangely confident. "Yeah, if you're paying."

He returned the smile. He raised his arm, signaling for the bartender, and when he got his attention, he ordered a classic margarita with no salt for Jamie, and a gin and tonic for himself. As the bartender retreated, the man turned his attention back to Jamie. "So it's you who's been out tipping my cows then, huh?"

"Oops, you caught me. So guilty."

She realized she was flirting. It had been so long since she flirted with someone that she almost didn't recognize it. It felt good, albeit foreign. She pushed her dark hair behind her ear, exposing her neck to him. Her eyes flitted to her cell phone, which had been silent for the past few minutes. She fought the urge to check it. Instead, she chanced another look at the stranger next to her. While he portrayed a sense of ease, of confidence, he seemed more anxious the longer Jamie looked. He picked at his fingernails. One of them was covered by a flesh-colored bandage that could use a change. One of his legs bounced rhythmically beneath the bar. He seemed distracted, eyes not resting on any one specific thing.

He hadn't asked her name yet, Jamie noticed.

The bartender returned moments later with the drinks, and as he walked away the man placed his credit card on the bar. Jamie normally wouldn't care to look, but her eyes were drawn to the unique combination of colors on the square of plastic: lime green with orange, arranged in a familiar swirl.

"Hey, you use Sprout," Jamie said, sipping her margarita. This one didn't taste as strong as the first one.

"Sprout?"

Jamie nodded. "Yeah, Sprout Credit Union. I work there." She shrugged. Almost immediately she regretted saying anything. She wasn't proud of her job. She hoped he wouldn't ask her questions about it.

"Oh." He smiled. "I do. Yeah, they have decent rates, I guess."

Jamie smoothed her hair down, fighting against the humidity in the club and continued. "Sorry, it's just a small bank and a lot of people don't use it. Most people opt for the United, I guess. They have the drive thru tellers there."

He didn't reply. He took a drink of his gin, eyes peering out into the rest of the bar as he drank. He seemed restless. Nervous. His throat bobbed as he swallowed hard. Jamie's eyes fell to the plastic again and noticed a strangely familiar word.

"Stoker?"

The word appeared to startle him. He frowned, eyes hardening as he turned directly to Jamie. "What?"

"Your last name," she said, gesturing with her chin to the card sitting between them. "As in Bram, right?"

He looked at the credit card. Relief appeared to flood through his body. His shoulders dropped and his brow softened. He reached his hand out and fingered the thin edges. With a humorless chuckle, he gently covered it with his hand.

"So what's your first name, Hannibal? Jason?" Jamie teased.

He took another drink, longer this time. "No, no," he said through a wry smile. "You know what?" He tried to mask his apparent discomfort. Jamie watched him flip the card over. "What if we," he continued, now connecting to Jamie with unwavering eye contact, "don't use our names?"

"No?"

"What if," he leaned in much closer, and Jamie could smell the thick herbal richness of his last cigarette on his breath, "we be anonymous tonight? No names."

Jamie stared blankly back. The man didn't break their gaze. This sudden eye contact felt heavy, implied. Her cheeks felt warm. She felt hot between her legs. She didn't realize she had been picking at her nails until she felt a pinch of pain at her cuticle, and then clamped her hands together to stop herself. With a thrill, Jamie realized that she knew exactly where things were headed. She hadn't been picked up in a bar in years. The mere idea turned her on. She wasn't the type to go home with someone she didn't know, a complete stranger, to risk safety and security for the excitement of anonymous sex. But a lot of things were new for her again, and the spontaneity of being as reckless as your nineteen-year-old self sent goosebumps down her arms.

Jamie felt her breath shallow, daring herself to say what she was about to say. Without breaking eye contact, she replied, "Well how will I know what name to scream?" She held her breath, awaiting either affirmation or rejection. *It's not too late*, she thought, *to play the whole thing off as a joke*.

He raised his eyebrows in mild surprise. He smiled, sitting back upright, and put his hands in his hair again.

"Do you want to come back to my place? I make a better gin and tonic, that's for sure." He drained the last of his drink and placed the empty glass back on the bar.

It was at that moment her phone buzzed.

The sudden vibration startled her. She turned the phone over and tapped the screen with her finger impatiently. She registered the message.

Don't be a bitch.

This time she shut off the phone and slid it into her bag.

"No, come with me, I live walking distance."

2.

From: Price, Carrie <carrie_the_one@firstmail.com>
To: Doe, Julie <anon821425@firstmail.com>
Sent: 30 March 2022, 5:52 p.m.
Subject: Re: Re: Information- DON'T DELETE

What makes you think I had anything to do with that? I don't even know who he is.

Carrie
Sent from my iPhone

JAMIE WALKED ALONGSIDE the man as the October air reddened their cheeks. The crisp wind whipped through their hair. Jamie spent the first block attempting to smooth hers down before eventually resigning to the tangles by the time they got to the gas station. She lived less than a ten-minute walk from BAR NEON and opted to walk today because the weather was so mild. However, now that the sun had been down for several hours, the temperature had plummeted and the general atmosphere was much more inhospitable. They walked against the wind, coats wrapped tightly over their chests, held firm by crossed arms. She was pissed at herself for not just driving.

Now with the frigid air in her face and her flush fading, she thought once more about what she was doing. She did not know this man, this man who wouldn't even tell her his name. And now they were outside on the street, walking alone, lit only by the neon and fluorescent lighting of neighboring storefronts. It was too early in the season for snow so their path along the cracked sidewalks was clear. There were, however, plenty of dry, browning leaves that floated on the wind in front of their feet. Jamie took pleasure in stepping on them as she walked, hearing that satisfying crunch crack through the silence.

They didn't say much. When they first left the bar, he cracked a joke about the cold, and then Jamie gave a quick description of which direction they were headed. After that the walk was mostly quiet, save for his question of if she lived alone. Jamie replied that she did. She didn't feel like giving the more complicated answer.

Now that the initial impulse had abated, Jamie's mind raced with all the logistical nightmares that came with an unexpected guest's arrival. When was the last time she cleaned the bathroom? Did she remember to put away that mound of clean laundry piled on the couch? She still had a sink full of dirty dishes that had been "soaking" for a day and a half. What underwear did she put on this morning?

Did she have any condoms left over from Alex?

She was on the pill, sure, but she didn't prefer to have sex without a condom, and something in her doubted that this guy had one on him. Briefly she considered stopping in at the pharmacy on the way, but then changed her mind. Something about stopping for a grocery run mid one-night stand was embarrassing, even as she convinced herself she was being irrational. If she didn't have a rubber at home, the pill would be fine, she concluded.

They got to Jamie's home a little after ten o'clock. As they approached her front walkway, she took the lead, walking slightly ahead, and dug in her pocket for her key. He stood closely behind her as, with trembling hands, she inserted the key into the lock and then pushed open the old door.

The two of them entered the home, and Jamie reached

behind to shut the door. As she turned the deadbolt, she felt a hand reach around to her belly. He pulled her up against him and buried his face in her hair. Jamie felt her heart race: arousal mixed with something else. She dropped her purse onto the floor. She felt one of his hands, still cold from the October air, push down past the waistband of her leggings and beneath the cotton of her underwear. Jamie's breath hitched as she allowed him to touch her, his fingers exploring her slick folds, warming to her heat. He didn't rub her clit, at least not intentionally, but she felt a pulse of desire radiate down from her belly button anyway. She leaned back against him, feeling his hardness against her ass. His other hand now snaked up under the hem of her shirt, creeping under her bra. He made contact with her bare breast, rolling her nipple between his fingers. His hands felt unpracticed, fumbling, and something about him led Jamie to believe he didn't have a lot of sex.

Suddenly he withdrew both hands and gripped her hips. He put his lips to her ear.

"Where's your room?" is all he said.

They toed out of their shoes and left them by the door. Jamie shrugged off her coat. As it fell, it encased her other belongings like some pillowy jellyfish. He, too, peeled off his coat.

She took him by the hand and led him to her bedroom. She was hyper aware of the dryness of his palm against the smoothness of hers, the push of her nipples against her bra, the heat rising in her ears. Passing through her kitchen, she eyed the pile of crusted dishes sitting in the sink, but he certainly didn't say anything. Once in her room, he shut the door firmly. No one turned on the light. The room was dark, only lit by the glow of the nearby streetlight out the window. For just a moment, the two stood at arms distance, and said nothing.

Now without his coat on, Jamie could see him fully. Separated from the bulk of his stiff outerwear, he seemed much smaller, shrunken. He was really barely any taller than she was. The light from outside cast a hard shadow on his face, exaggerating the sunken flesh of his under eyes. The hollows of his cheeks. It seemed to alter his face altogether, and although his expression didn't change, Jamie felt a pang of fear. Now only in his wrinkled t-shirt, his bare arms were entirely exposed. With unease, she noticed several dark, roundish marks embedded in the soft skin of his biceps and trailing down to his forearm. Jamie couldn't tell how many were there. In the dim room, she couldn't distinguish if they were bruises or scabs or something else, but the sight made her shiver. She needed to know what they were.

She moved to the lamp, arm reaching to switch it on, until—

"No."

She froze, arm outstretched, waiting for more.

He closed the space between them, took her by the arm, and spun her to face him. His grasp was strong, but it didn't hurt.

"No, leave them off."

He took her face in his hands and covered her mouth with his. He was rough. Jamie recoiled at the scratch of facial hair on her nose, her chin, but he clung tight. He moved his hands to the back of her head, holding her to him. Jamie muffled something between a protest and a plea to slow down, bringing her hands to his wrists. She kissed him back but wasn't sure why. She didn't feel turned on anymore. The backs of her knees were flat against the edge of her bed.

Lowering his hands to her shoulders, he pressed her down against the bed, mouth still covering hers.

He didn't ask about a condom.

He ran his hands down her throat, and over her breasts, still covered by her shirt. Jamie didn't know what to do with her hands. They remained partially clenched, up near her face. She tried to press her palms against his chest, wanting to feel the warmth of his skin beneath his shirt, but he shrugged her away. He didn't seem to want to be touched. He moved quickly, purposefully, eyes barely looking where his fingers roamed. He positioned himself between her legs and leaned up to hook his fingers into her waistband. He peeled the leggings off in one motion, leaving a perfect snakeskin behind.

"What's your name?" she asked, searching for something, anything.

He didn't reply.

He pressed his body onto hers, mouth roaming the skin of her neck. Jamie felt his fingers caressing her through the fabric of her underwear, and then slipping a finger inside. She felt herself go slick, hot. She closed her eyes with the sensation. As he rubbed her, she felt the sensation build as she grew tighter and tighter, a piano wire stretched to its limit. She wanted him to stop, but she wanted him to touch her, just like that, just a minute longer.

The pressure stopped. He pulled away, and pulled down the fabric, now wet with her. Jamie arched her back off the bed, allowing for room to do so. He tossed them aside, into the dark unknown of her room. Now totally exposed from the waist down, she felt goosebumps erupt along the flesh of her legs. No sooner had she wriggled out of her underwear—she had forgotten to check what she had been wearing, it hardly seemed to matter to anyone—that he pushed up onto his knees, unzipped his jeans, pulled himself out.

He pushed into her with no preamble, and Jamie gasped.

He stabilized himself with his arms, one on either side of Jamie's head, and thrust into her repeatedly. His movements didn't hurt, but they didn't feel good either. They felt obligatory, mechanical. He didn't touch her anywhere else; in fact, he seemed intent on touching her as little as possible. He said nothing. He didn't look at her.

His movements were frantic, hurried. She wasn't even sure he was enjoying himself.

A car drove by outside. As it did, the headlights cast a mad blaze of yellow light into the room, against the walls, and then harshly across the man's face. It underlit him for the briefest of moments, reminding Jamie of her summer camp days, where campers would take turns wielding flashlights under chins, mid-ghost-story, huddled around a simmering campfire. The headlight illuminated something else, too. She saw the unexplained marks on the inside of his arms, close to her face. With disgust, she realized they were swollen, purulent sores. They looked painful and angry. The nearest one was inches from her nose, and she imagined it bursting and oozing down into her exposed eye. Nausea rose in her gut. Jamie looked up at him as he fucked her. His brow was damp, eyes squeezed shut. He wasn't with her in her bedroom at all, he was someplace far away. It was like he wanted to get it over with as soon as possible, Jamie thought.

She could tell he was about to come. His thrusts became faster, more urgent. With no other sounds in the room, the slap of their damp flesh repeatedly making contact seemed as loud as gunshots. The arms that held him steady off the bed, Jamie could feel them begin to quiver. His eyes were still pressed closed, the lines between his eyebrows deep. In between gasps, Jamie thought she could make out a word. Words? One repeated syllable, murmured, like a choked prayer.

"Please, please, please."

Jamie looked up in horror, beside herself, yet afraid to know more. His movements were hard, desperate, and with a final strangled cry, he stopped moving, tight muscles going slack.

He went limp, allowing the full weight of his body to rest on top of her. He panted, hard and fast, fighting against his lungs to breathe. Jamie felt his body damp through the fabric of his t-shirt, and now smelled from him the musky scent of a skipped shower.

He rolled off of Jamie, and she was suddenly cold and exposed. Between her legs she felt wetness puddling onto her sheets. She reached for her bedsheet that was crumpled at the foot of her bed still, having never been made this morning. Neither said anything. Jamie turned her head slightly to look at the man. He stared up at the bedroom ceiling. He didn't look sated, at peace, or even comfortable. He placed a hand on his forehead, pausing as if checking for fever. His breathing slowed, and the cool air of the room dried the sweat from his skin. Jamie snuck another look at his arms, and this time, he met her gaze. He saw her looking and pulled his arm close to his body.

Just as Jamie was about to say something, he rolled off the bed, stood, put himself away, and zipped his pants up. Jamie sat up in bed and watched him move to the bedroom door.

He picked up his strewn shirt and turned to her. "Alright, have a good night."

He opened the door and disappeared into the darkness of her hallway. She heard the shuffling of a coat, the clunk of a pair of boots, the jingle of a set of keys, and then the opening of her front door.

And then the closing of her front door.

And then he was gone.

3.

Do you have it?

Carrie
Sent from my iPhone

JAMIE FELT TWO ways about it.

Mostly she felt confused. The whole evening was weird, from their meeting to his refusal to give Jamie any personal information, and then to her walking him to her front door. And the sex was unlike any sex she had ever had. It felt weird. Now, she hardly considered herself to be the epitome of human sexual experience; she didn't lose her virginity until she was nineteen, and since then had only had a handful of partners. She was sure there was a lot of weird sex to be had in the world. Maybe she felt a bit prideful, too? Was it a little exciting to have done something so risky, so impulsive, and with minimal regard for self-preservation? After all, she was initially turned on by the concept of anonymous sex. Wasn't this what she wanted? Everyone has weird sexual encounters every once in a while, she reasoned. She was hardly the first and wouldn't be the last. Still, despite her best efforts to convince herself otherwise, she also felt somewhat violated, taken advantage of. She had been an open and willing participant, sure, but his urgency, his lack of attention to her needs, and his cavalier and swift exit from her room just echoed tasteless and cheap.

Jamie didn't have a clock in her bedroom, and her phone was still in her bag, so she didn't know the time. However, she knew it was too early to sleep, and she felt too alive, too wired for rest. She pushed herself out of the bed. After a brief search, she retrieved her discarded underwear from the floor and put them on. She didn't want to dirty a fresh pair yet, not until she had the opportunity to shower.

She stripped off the shirt she had been wearing, and replaced it with an oversized, hole riddled t-shirt from her dresser drawer. It was her favorite: a free handout from Welcome Week of Freshman year at State. She arrived to campus late, and by the time she had checked in, there was only one box of 3XLs left, and she was forced to take one. She felt slighted during orientation. All of the other girls wore their campus shirts fitted, showing off their figures, their tits, while Jamie was forced to wear hers tucked deeply into her jeans, the fabric chunking into her waistband and billowing up and over like some alien cotton mushroom. But now she'd had it so long and washed it so many times that the cotton had thinned and softened to the smoothest, most buttery texture. The denim color had faded over the years, the armpits and collar were freckled with holes that opened more and more with each new wear and wash. This shirt was the longest relationship she'd had with anything.

She exited the room and went to the kitchen to make herself a cup of tea. For a moment she considered texting Frankie. She could really use a female friend to process things with, and Frankie was sort of it. Jamie's job kept her pretty isolated, and the only coworkers she really interacted with were either working their way through college, or about to hit retirement. In fact, she couldn't remember the last time anyone other *than* Frankie had set foot in her home as a guest.

The thought suddenly occurred to Jamie that the discomforting guy she just let have sex with her knew where she lived.

Nothing about his demeanor particularly screamed "threat," but the fact remained. Something deep in her gut reacted viscerally to that knowledge, and a slick bubble of nausea rose inside her.

She turned, headed for the phone still stuffed in her bag by the front door, and as she did, she passed her oven. Her eyes registered the time on the digital clock, and she stopped. Frankie had Sunday clinic hours tomorrow and was probably already in bed. Jamie decided not to bother her. Everything was fine. She was getting herself excited for nothing. Instead, she resumed making tea.

As she filled her electric kettle with water from the tap, she heard a knock at the front door.

She froze, and her heart thumped in her throat.

Is that him again? Jamie's own voice screamed in her ears. *What does he want with me?* she asked herself irrationally. She felt her heart beat in her temples, violently rhythmic, in time with the thumping in her chest. Jamie realized she was holding her breath. Why would he be back? Her feet were lead, but she shuffled them forward nonetheless. She crossed through the kitchen and into the living room and scanned the space. Did he leave something behind? A phone? A wallet? Nothing seemed out of order.

Another quick series of knocks echoed through her home.

She very well couldn't pretend she wasn't home. *It's probably nothing, just go see what he wants.* Jamie inched toward the door, and as she approached cursed the fact that she didn't have a peephole. She grasped the knob and pulled open the door.

It wasn't the man at all. It was Alex.

Alex was tall and broad-shouldered. He wore a thickly lined flannel jacket and lived-in denim jeans tucked into his work boots. The two of them shared eye contact, and he shifted his weight, the movement pronounced by the jingling of his keys hooked into his belt loop. His thumbs were tucked into his back pockets. He looked annoyed. The shock of seeing him must have been all over Jamie's face. Alex raised his hands in a "Surprise!" gesture. He wore a smile, but there was no humor in his eyes.

"What are you doing here?"

Alex sighed. "I've been texting you all evening."

He had been. In reality, he had been messaging her for days. Texting was one way to say it. Another way was harassment. However, she wasn't in the mood to fend off an argument, so she tempered her response. "I know."

"So why haven't you answered?"

"My phone's been off, it's in my bag." It wasn't technically a lie.

Alex seemed to turn her reply over in his head. Jamie wondered if he was going to ask to see inside her purse, and she was prepared to show him. Instead, he asked, "Who was that guy?"

The sudden shift in topic caught Jamie off guard, and she meant it when she replied, "What? Who?"

"That guy I just saw leave." He pointed over his shoulder with a thumb.

Jamie was stricken with horror. The idea that Alex could have been watching her, following her, had never crossed her mind. She felt a chill that had nothing to do with the open doorway she was standing in. She crossed her arms over her chest, hugging herself for warmth. She was suddenly very aware of how little she actually had on. She was completely exposed. "Have you been sitting outside of my house?"

"No." He smirked, leaning against the door frame. He clearly enjoyed whatever game he was playing.

"You know, I should call the goddamn cops."

"Relax." He rolled his eyes. "I just got here. Just in time to see Johnny Bravo walk out of here with a little pep in his step."

"Alex. We aren't together anymore, remember?"

At that, he closed the space between them, and began to push his way into the house.

Jamie put a hand on his chest but was hyper aware that she couldn't actually restrain him if he tried to push past her. "What are you doing?"

"I'm freezing my balls off out here."

"Good, they could use a break," she retorted, uncharacteristically brazen for an interaction with Alex. He had the tendency to react disproportionately to humor, especially if he sensed he was the butt of the joke.

"Har har. Will you fucking let me in or what?" His face was mere inches from hers. His breath smelled sour and she wrinkled her nose against the odor.

Jamie sighed. She weighed the option of giving in with the annoyance of having to verbally spar with him here, halfway out in the cold. The goosebumps on her legs protested the temperature. She knew she was going to need to go back in, and Alex wasn't going anywhere anytime soon, at least not until he wanted to. She took a step back, allowing him entrance.

"Fine. Just don't try anything."

"Yeah, right, as if I want Fonzie's sloppy seconds."

She chose to ignore the remark. She headed back to the kitchen and he followed behind. He didn't bother to remove his boots.

"I was just about to make some tea. Want a cup?" She opened her mug cupboard and grasped the handle of the first one she touched, waiting for the indication if she should retrieve just one mug or two.

Alex leaned against the island and stretched his neck from side to side. "I don't suppose you have any Tito's, huh?"

"Nope," she replied, leaning over into her open tea bag canister, observing its contents, "but I do have Earl Grey, Green Tea, Peppermint, Chai, and at least one Wild Berry."

"I'll pass then," he grinned.

"You sure? Because the sooner you warm up, the sooner you'll be on your way."

"Calm down, I'll be out of your hair in a few."

As she busied herself with her kettle, selected her tea bag, and gathered her sugar jar, Alex took his phone out and fiddled with it, clearly doing nothing in particular.

Jamie didn't delude herself into believing that she'd never have to see Alex again. They had dated for a brief but tumultuous six months, and things ended as quickly as they began. They met at work; he came in seeking a personal loan to buy a new truck, and each appointment ended with him asking Jamie for her number. Each time, with a polite smile, she'd refuse. He was cute and earnest and the two had an immediate electric energy. They'd trade quips over stacks of paper, attempting to find the balance between wisecracks and faxing W-2s. But as Jamie was in charge of handling the underwriting, she simply wasn't comfortable pursuing anything more.

By the time they closed the loan, she had agreed to give him her number. A week later she agreed to go out with him. Things were intense in the beginning. Their banter became like foreplay; they'd throw out playful insults with the intent of challenging the other to come up with an equally snappy reply, and then back and forth over and over until their clothes were in an indistinguishable pile on the floor and at least one of them was pressed against the nearest private wall.

But over time, things changed. Their banter became less flirty and more spiteful. Their words became weapons. The sex became less of an enthusiastic team event and more of an individual means to an end. Pretty soon Jamie realized that once she peeled away all the sex and the dry humor and the verbal foreplay, there wasn't anything left. But even that wasn't the final straw.

"I'd actually like to finish our conversation," Alex said suddenly, refocusing Jamie's attention to the kitchen at large. She had thoughtlessly scooped too much sugar into her mug and had to pour some back out.

"What conversation?" Jamie frowned, dusting excess sugar off of her counter, and then filling her mug with boiling water.

"The conversation I was trying to have when messaging you tonight."

Jamie turned and faced him. "We weren't having a conversation," she pointed out.

Alex pushed off the island and took a step toward her. "You've been ghosting me for a week."

"Can you think of a reason why I might be doing that?"

"That's what I've been trying to find out."

She scoffed, turned back, and began steeping her tea bag into the hot water. She stood over the steam, and let the moist heat sink into her cheeks. Her mounting resentment spread a new heat, an ugly heat, up her neck and into her ears. Was the inevitable resulting argument worth the snide impulse bubbling in her throat?

"How's Liz by the way?" she said, coolly.

Alex was quiet. She could tell he was calculating a reply. In a rare moment of vulnerability, Alex simply wasn't prepared for Jamie to have known. She lifted the tea to her lips and took a sip. She didn't give him the satisfaction of turning to face him.

Finally, he replied. "Oh, you know about her, huh?" He tried his best to come across unbothered, even cavalier, but Jamie knew him well enough to know he was frantically searching for a way out.

"Yep. I know about her."

He scoffed. "I don't know who you're talking to to get this—"

"And Paige?"

Alex barked out a humorless laugh. "Shit you think you're smart, don't you? What, you think you know something?" His voice was loud and bitter, completely void of all the charm it had possessed only moments prior. "Will you turn around and look at me?"

Jamie turned. She held her hot mug close to her body, like a tiny shield. Alex placed himself on the other side of the island, as though he couldn't stand being too close to Jamie. His face was deeply red, and he feverishly shifted his weight side to side, working out what else there was to say.

"You know," he spat out from behind a discomforting smile, "You have a lot of room to talk."

Jamie frowned. "What does that mean?"

"That guy." He pointed vaguely in the direction of the front door. "Did you fuck him? Or did you just play Monopoly?"

"Well you know I've got to play catch up. When we were together, I wasn't having sex nearly as often as you were."

"Oh, that's hilarious. That's funny." He stopped pacing and directly squared off his shoulders to face Jamie. "So how long *has* it been going on, since you're so high and mighty?"

"Get over yourself, I only just met the guy."

"What, tonight?" he spat, incredulously. "Shit I had to work on you for two weeks before you'd even let me finger you, and here this douche gets it in after he, what, sits and listens to your sad mom story one time?"

For several seconds, she was stricken, incredulous as to how to respond. They hadn't known one another very long before they started dating, but Alex still knew precisely how to hurt her, and wasn't afraid to do so.

"Alex, I don't owe you anything," Jamie said, moving to exit the kitchen. She was starting to feel trapped in, and Alex was scaring her. She had never seen him like this, and she felt uncomfortable not having her phone on her. Alex was much taller and much stronger than she was, and he could so easily overpower her. The panic that she had denied herself swam in her guts.

As she moved, Alex directly countered, meeting Jamie in two long strides and planting himself directly in her path. Mere inches separated them. Jamie refused to look him in his eyes, focusing her gaze on a vague spot on his shoulder instead. However, she felt his eyes penetrating directly into her skull, boring into bone, daring her to look up. She refused. She clutched her mug so tightly her knuckles began to cramp. She wildly thought of throwing the hot liquid in his face, and as if reading her mind, Alex grabbed Jamie's wrist, holding her to the spot.

"You don't think I could get you back?" His free hand stroked a feather touch down Jamie's side, fingering the hem of her old shirt. It wasn't sexual. It was threatening. Controlling.

Jamie wrenched free from his grip. "I think it's time for you to go."

She weaved around him and went to the front door. She didn't like that he was behind her, out of her sightlines, but he wasn't going to leave of his own volition. She unlocked the door, swung it open, and stood back, waiting for him. The bitter cold shocked Jamie's bare legs, but she refused to let Alex see it affect her. She stood firm in the doorway and sipped her tea, despite her utter lack of wanting it anymore. Alex leered at her from the kitchen entry, and for a moment, Jamie was really worried that she was going to have to call the cops.

In a final act of desperation, Jamie sighed. "I'm going to spend tomorrow going through some of my mom's old stuff and I want to get some sleep." She had hoped to sound resigned, tired. Reasonable. She hoped to appeal to whatever level of sensibility he still possessed.

He crossed into the living room and approached the door. He put a hand on the handle. "I'm gonna text you tomorrow, and you need to answer," he said.

"Don't come back here."

He shut the door forcefully behind him. Jamie immediately locked it. Her face was still hot, and she blinked away the sting forming in her eyes. She pressed her ear against the door, eyes squeezed shut. She held her breath, listening for whatever sounds she could. She heard heavy footsteps retreating. The jingle of keys. The start of an engine. Headlights spilled in through the window of her dining room, and then turned out of sight. Exhaling, Jamie felt the anger slowly receding. She had had enough of this day. She leaned down and shuffled through her purse, retrieving her phone, and turned it back on.

It was just about midnight, and she felt the exhaustion of the day deep in her bones. The muscles between her shoulders were tight, and she felt a headache creeping into the pulp behind her eyes. She was going to take some Tylenol, have a shower, and go right to sleep.

Passing through her bedroom, she picked a fresh pair of underwear from her dresser drawer—a nothing pair of white cotton—and made her way to the hall bathroom. She plucked a clean towel from the linen closet and set the items to balance on the sink. Her skin felt grimy, unclean with the sweat of a stranger, and she wanted to be free of it. She felt a sick alien urge to peel off her skin like an old sock and hang it from the towel hook above her. She reached a hand into the shower and turned the water on hot.

As she waited for the stream to heat to a proper scald, Jamie realized she needed to pee. She stepped over to the toilet, pulled down her underwear, and sat. The urine came in a hot, high-pressure gush, and Jamie sighed in relief. She didn't realize how badly she had to go. God, she was so tired, she could just fall asleep here on the toilet, lulled by the rushing water and the rising steam heat. She rubbed her hands forcefully up and down her face, trying to encourage blood flow. Needing to wake up. Jamie dropped her hands and blinked away the little stars popping in her vision. The room came back into focus and her eyes drifted downward. She noticed something unusual, and stared at the space between her knees. Brows furrowed. Doing math in her head. *My period isn't due for another week*, she thought.

There, slung between the crooks of both knees, soaked into the very center of her underwear, was blood.

4.

From: Price, Carrie <carrie_the_one@firstmail.com>
To: Doe, Julie <anon821425@firstmail.com>
Sent: 2 April 2022, 2:42 p.m.
Subject: Fine I'll tell you

So I've thought it over and I've decided you've got just as much to lose as I have if you run to the cops. Don't think your stupid sock puppet email is actually protecting you, if I ever needed to find out who you were. Not to sound like a raving bitch, but I'm sure you've figured out by now how desperate I can get if I'm backed into a corner. And since I also get the feeling you won't leave me alone until you know more, I'll give you what you want. I have a good life, all of this is behind me now, and I don't need you showing up at my door anytime soon.

Let me get to a desktop because there's a lot to tell.

Carrie
Sent from my iPhone

EVEN BEFORE WAKING, Jamie knew she had slept in. The light that shone through her window was far too bright and direct for it to be any time close to morning. She guessed it had to be approaching noon. As Jamie settled into consciousness, she took notice of her body. Stiffness held her body in a vice grip. Fighting the discomfort of movement, she rolled herself up and out of bed and slung her legs over the edge of the mattress. There, she spent a few moments kneading her shoulders with her knuckles and rolling the tension out of her neck. The ache radiated down into her lower back, and she stretched against the tightness. She pinched her nose between two fingers and exhaled. A headache, too. Great. She made a mental note that one-night stands and tequila at the hot new bar might just be part of her past.

She wiggled her toes into the fibers of her carpet, stood, shuffled to the bathroom, and sat to pee.

Fresh confusion struck her at the sight of new blood on her toilet paper. Her period was rarely irregular, and it was never this early. Mentally calculating, she hadn't noticed any soreness or cramping that usually indicated the start of her cycle. Normally her breasts would be heavy and sore, and her lower back would ache for days. She'd have a night or two of restless sleep. Plus, she was on the pill, which forced her cycle to stay on schedule. However, she reminded herself of the pain she woke up with today, and determining that the puzzle pieces fit, Jamie came to the conclusion that, yes, her period had simply just come early. Annoying, yes, but not dire. She reached over to the cabinet under her sink, pulled out a pad, and stuck it in her underwear.

In the kitchen, she brewed coffee and prepared toast. As she scooped the stale grounds into the paper filter, she picked up her phone. She swiped away the unread messages left by Alex and scrolled to Frankie's name. She typed *hey I know you work the weekend, but when you get a moment shoot me a text. I need to tell you what happened last night* and then put the phone back down on the counter.

Jamie and Frankie met in college. Jamie was halfway through her communications program and Frankie was in her last year of her bio degree, prepping Physician

Assistant program applications for the coming fall. They had a shared elective, Intro to Philosophical Concepts, which they had both chosen to wait to take. Early in the semester, they were paired together for an in-class discussion, and as Frankie approached Jamie's seat and slumped into the chair, she turned to Jamie and said, "How do you get a philosophy grad off your porch? You pay him for the pizza." She cracked open the textbook. "I hate philosophy."

Frankie was effortlessly cool with dark black hair and a heavy bang that hung below her eyebrows. She wore the same yellow framed eyeglasses and pair of classic high-top Converses every day. She drank her coffee black and could internet-stalk anyone with the least possible information. She spoke with the utmost self-confidence. Jamie liked her instantly. They were both locals with families close by, but despite their fantasies about running away and never returning, neither actually planned to stray too far. Jamie stayed close for her mother, and Frankie stayed out of duty to her education. She was at school on a full scholarship, something she wasn't granted anywhere else. If she had been, she would have been three states away by now. So while Jamie went home every weekend to see her mom, Frankie had to be pried out of her apartment to go home for Christmas break.

Jamie's phone buzzed. Frankie's reply: *With who, Alex?*

No, well sort of. Jamie couldn't deny that Alex was part of the story, but she was planning to lead with the mystery man and BAR NEON.

I thought you were over him and his bullshit, Frankie sent back.

That's not what I mean. Don't you have patients or something?

Frankie worked at a smallish but stable family practice about fifteen minutes up the road, so although they didn't see one another very often, she never felt too far away.

When she joined the practice a couple years back, Jamie was surprised. She assumed Frankie would be on the first flight to New York or San Francisco after she passed licensing, but as it turns out, her internship supervisor had a connection to a position opening at the clinic, and Frankie couldn't pass up a sure thing right out of school. It was great news for Jamie, though. She dreaded the thought of having to meet new people. She already met her person. They knew each other's stories. They had introduced one another to their favorite movies, and read each other's favorite books. Plus, Frankie was chronically addicted to her phone, so she was always reachable.

You know how it is, the Sunday crowd looking for any reason to get an excuse slip for work tomorrow morning.

Jamie grinned at her phone, then typed her own response: *Hell yeah go make that money. We'll talk later.*

Ok byeee.

Jamie's big plans to graduate college and move away to go work for a large marketing firm were quickly foiled after her mom was diagnosed with cancer. Her doctor caught it quickly, but early detection aside, it wasn't a pleasant kind, and wasn't a kind most people walked away from. Her mother was single and an only child, so there weren't a lot of options in terms of support when she got sick. Jamie went home often during the semesters and spent every holiday with her mother. Her mother was fine for a while, until she wasn't.

Soon after graduation, Jamie moved back home permanently.

Near the end she was her mother's sole caregiver—because who else did they have? Jamie certainly couldn't hire a nurse or arrange for a long-term care facility, so she took on the responsibility. She took her mom to all her treatments, the ones her insurance would cover anyway, and assumed the daily tasks of cooking, cleaning, fixing the car, and paying the bills. As her mother's body began to fall apart, Jamie was there to feed her, clean her, and change her diapers. But that wasn't nearly as terrible as when her mind began to fall apart.

Jamie watched her mother, once a tough, sturdy, fuck-around-and-find-out sort of woman, simply disintegrate like wet tissue in a clenched palm. In the beginning she forgot little things, like where she had placed the remote, or how old Jamie was turning that summer. These things usually gave the pair a chuckle, the cause of no worry. Real red flags began to go off when her mother struggled to remember who Jamie was, despite her now living with her. At the end, she stopped speaking. Her eyes stared, glazed over, into nothing. She became something that wasn't Jamie's mother.

Her mother died just over a year ago. Jamie inherited her childhood home, the small two-bedroom Ranch with the unfinished basement, and lived there ever since. Although Jamie had owned the property since her mom's death, she hadn't put in much effort toward updating the home. Touches of her mother were everywhere. She ate off the same plates. She sat on the same furniture. She used the same bath towels. Jamie still hadn't emptied out her mother's old room, including her closets and storage space, so now it sat empty, a corpse itself.

Her grief was partly the reason she was drawn to Alex in the first place. She was vulnerable, depressed, and willing to accept any external validation that she could get. He slipped into her life at the most opportune moment and gutted her from the inside out.

She decided that she would start gradually working her way through her mother's belongings. She wasn't sure she was ever going to move out of the second bedroom and into the master, but she admitted to herself that she could use the extra space. The house was small, just barely cracking 1,000 square feet, and immediately losing one room to the ghost of her mother made Jamie feel even more constricted.

She refilled her coffee mug, rescued a pile of flattened cardboard boxes from the recycling bin, hoisted them up under her arm, and disappeared into her mother's old room.

A couple hours later, she had to take a break. She had taken down and folded most of the clothing into donation boxes, electing to keep a couple of her mother's cozier cardigans for herself. Jamie wasn't highly sentimental, but she was comforted by the idea of wrapping herself in her mother's clothing if it meant feeling close to her for that one moment. No one else would know except her, and she would be able to keep her grief private. Her mother's shoes were all destined for donations, and Jamie had tossed all the undergarments in the trash. She started to empty out the nightstand tables, mostly filled with junk, and stripped the bed of its old linens. She had even gotten to finally fold the clean laundry pile that had been mounting on her living room couch, awaiting attention. But now she worried she had overdone things. Her lower back and abdomen were throbbing in pain, and she had already changed out her pad twice. She sat down on the floor of her mom's room and tried to ride out the next cramp.

"Holy fucking shit," she sputtered through gritted teeth, eyes squeezed shut. Her organs twisted tight in a vice grip, leaving her breathless. She pulled her knees close to her chest and breathed against the throbbing of a migraine now developing deep in her eye sockets. She suddenly had to pee. Jamie stood, and hobbled past the master bathroom she never used, down the hall, and into the bathroom just outside her bedroom.

The very moment she sat on the toilet and began to urinate, she was struck with violent sharpness. She yelled out and clenched her knees together, stricken by the white-hot pain of a fire poker being inserted inside her.

"Fuck!" she exclaimed. She had very little to brace

herself against, so she gripped the sides of the seat, praying for her bladder to empty as quickly as possible. The hot urine continued to release in a powerful stream, and as it did the shock of pain persisted. Her heart was in her throat and she felt her nails bend against her grip on the porcelain. Gradually she finished and the pain receded.

She slid off the seat and came to a kneeling position on the tile. Her bangs stuck to the slick wetness of her forehead, and the back of her tee shirt was damp to the touch. Her underwear tangled at her ankles. She looked down and saw that her pad was once again totally saturated, and gracelessly stuck to the inside of her calf.

"What the fuck was that?" she breathed, peeling it off and dropping it in her trash can. She had never experienced that amount of pain while pissing. She turned toward the bowl and saw the entirety of the toilet water was a deep, bloody red. She dabbed herself clean with a wad of toilet paper, replaced the pad, and flushed the toilet. Still riding out the aftershocks of the cramp, Jamie lay down on the bathroom floor, cheek pressed against the cool tile, and closed her eyes.

It was still early, barely dinner, by the time Jamie decided she had had enough and put herself to bed. She didn't get a lot more work done in her mom's room in between the continued cramping pains, but she did manage to collect the boxes for donation and bring them to the front door, ready to be driven to the thrift shop. In a wild moment, during another episode, she considered calling for an ambulance, but buried that idea at the thought of paying for even a fraction of what that bill might be. So instead, she swallowed a small palmful of extra strength Tylenol, went to her bed, and wrapped herself in her comforter, simultaneously freezing and boiling hot.

She stuck a hand out from beneath the blanket and dialed Frankie's number.

"Hey," Frankie answered, a question in her voice. They almost exclusively talked over text, and for one to call the other was at the very least unusual, and at the worst an utter emergency. But Jamie wasn't in the mood to type out her every thought, and her eyes hurt too badly to stare at a bright screen, so she called instead.

"Hey," Jamie replied, aware of how weak her voice sounded. "Listen, do you have time to see me tomorrow?"

She sensed alarm in Frankie's voice. "Why? What's wrong?" Jamie rarely went to the doctor, and never sought medical advice from Frankie.

"I don't know, I don't feel great."

"Well what's going on?"

What *was* going on? Jamie didn't know. She felt sick in every possible way but lacked the medical literacy to explain most of it. "I'm in a lot of pain," she began. "My back hurts, and it burns when I piss. I think I'm getting a fever, too."

"What happened?"

Jamie sighed. This wasn't how she had planned for this conversation to go. She wanted to gab with Frankie over coffee or while out getting lunch, spilling the gory details in between bites of a BLT and attempting to find the stranger's profile online somewhere. From there, they'd talk shit on him amongst themselves, cackling into their sandwiches, and Frankie would roll her eyes at the lame lines that worked on Jamie. Instead, Jamie relayed her symptoms clinically and devoid of any humor, teeth chattering against the chill she felt in her skin. "I slept with a new guy. I think I got a UTI or something, I don't know, I don't get them a lot."

"Is this what you wanted to talk about earlier? What guy?"

"Frankie, can you see me tomorrow or not?" She didn't mean to come across as irritable as she sounded.

"Listen," Frankie sighed, worry etching her words, "do you need to go to the ER? I can come pick you up if you need me."

"No, no, I took some Tylenol. I'm gonna call off work tomorrow. Can I just come into the office in the morning? Do you have time? I really want to avoid the ER."

She heard a series of clicks come through over Frankie's line. They had the distinct *ping* of a desktop mouse. Jamie envisioned Frankie clicking through a schedule.

"Yeah," Frankie replied, "I have time. Can you get here for ten?"

Jamie sighed with relief. "Yeah."

"Okay, good. We'll see what's going on."

"Thank you."

"Are you sure you don't need an emergency room? You sound awful, James."

"I'm sure. Listen, I'm gonna go. I'm going to bed, hopefully I can sleep off some of this fever at least and feel better tomorrow." She wrapped her blanket tighter around her shoulders.

"Yeah, maybe," Frankie said, not sounding convinced. "Just promise me you'll go to the hospital if you feel worse, okay?"

"I will," Jamie lied.

They said goodbye. Jamie ended the call and was asleep immediately.

5.

It all started with a guy.

I know, I know. What a fucking cliché. I don't need it told to me, I already know. I hate seeing it typed out like this almost as much as I hate thinking it. But it's the truth. I'm giving you total honesty. This is all because of some absolute seeping pustule I once dated named Ethan. There's no point in trying to hide it. Considering you found me, I'm sure by now you know who he was. I hate that I was so stupid with him, and I hate it even more that I allowed him to get under my skin the way he did. No fucking man is worth the hassle. But I learned that too late, I guess.

Carrie

THE NEXT DAY, Jamie didn't feel much better, but she was able to roll out of bed, put on a fresh set of clothing, and get out the door in time. On the way out, she made sure to grab the bottle of Tylenol and take it with her. Fuck her screaming liver, she wasn't going to get through the morning without it.

In the car she texted her boss, letting him know she was sick and going to the doctor. He didn't usually give her a lot of grief for taking time off, which was a relief considering how much time she was forced to take while caring for her mom. She was rounding the corner of five years of employment with Sprout, and as such had built up a decent relationship with her boss. He trusted her to not abuse their call off system. He was a good man, and Jamie appreciated him. Not all are.

Five minutes before her appointment time, Jamie pulled up to the building. The practice sat right in the middle of a business park, sharing one large parking lot with another primary care office, a dentist, a pizza shop, a post office, and a grocery store. Thankfully the palmful of Tylenol she took this morning was kicking in some; the cramps had abated a bit, and the nausea-inducing headache dulled to a mere throb. Jamie gingerly stepped out of the car. She approached the large gray sign that hung on the red brick exterior beside the front door:

CHUTNEY HEIGHTS PRIMARY CARE

On the sign was a list of a few of the practice's providers, and there, listed second from the bottom was FRANCESCA MACHER PA-C.

Inside at the welcome desk, Jamie signed in, handed over her insurance card for scanning, and filled out the demographic papers. She was called back before completing them, so as she shuffled down the hall in the nurse's wake, Jamie continued feverishly scribbling on the cracked clipboard. Once in the room, the nurse retrieved the clipboard, took Jamie's vital signs, and handed her a small plastic cup for her piss. Jamie filled the cup in the bathroom, which was again tinged a discomforting pink color, and returned to the exam room. Fifteen minutes later, Frankie entered.

"You slut," she grinned, closing the door behind her.

"Hey, Frank," Jamie grimaced.

Even in professional wear, she looked cool. She wore a deep purple button down tucked into a pair of tailored black trousers, and her dark hair was pulled back into a low pony. Today's eyeglasses were lime green. She vaguely held up a printout of what Jamie had to assume were her test results.

"I mean yeah, it looks like you have a UTI." She shrugged, eyes scanning the document. "Your white blood cells are elevated, so there's definitely an infection someplace. Given that, with your dysuria, abdominal and flank pain and recent," she wiggled her eyebrows, "new sexual partner, it makes sense clinically."

"So, is that it?"

Frankie crossed her arms and leaned up against the door. "I mean I'll send out a culture on it but yeah, your urine lit up like a Christmas tree. I'll send a script for an antibiotic over to your pharmacy. You should start feeling better in a couple of days," she said, matter-of-factly.

"Good because I feel like dog shit now."

"Yeah you look it, too." She snapped on a pair of blue latex gloves, reached over Jamie's head, and picked up the ophthalmoscope from the wall. She shined the light into Jamie's eye and leaned in close.

"So, what about my period?" Jamie asked, squinting in the light.

"Don't blink. What about it?"

"Well, it's over a week early and I've been bleeding like crazy. It's really heavy."

"Are you still on the pill?" She switched to Jamie's other eye.

Jamie nodded. "I never went off."

"I mean," Frankie said, shrugging, "UTIs really don't affect the menstrual cycle but we can have some blood work sent out and order an ultrasound." She hung the scope back up on the wall. "But gyno's not really my specialty, so I'd tell you to see yours."

Jamie probably should have admitted she hadn't seen a gynecologist in years, but didn't say anything.

"So," Frankie said, settling into a chair directly across from Jamie and crossing one leg over the other, "tell me about your new guy."

"Are you sure you can talk about it now? Like don't you have patients?"

"Oh," Frankie replied, waving her hand dismissively, "I rescheduled someone to get you in and I don't have anyone for another twenty."

"Are you allowed to do that?"

Frankie shrugged. "Sure. Besides, my nurse can handle anything that pops up. Anyway, talk! Give me the dirty details." She rested her chin in her open palm eagerly.

Jamie picked at her cuticles and fiddled with her fingers. She swayed her legs absentmindedly as they dangled off the side of the exam table. "I definitely wouldn't consider him 'my guy.' I don't know, now that I'm dealing with this, it all seems a little less fun to dish about."

Frankie waited, expectedly.

Jamie knew Frankie would just continue to wait her out, so she blurted out in one breath, "I went to BAR NEON the other night and I met him and then he came back to my house and we had sex. It was weird and I really didn't have a good time and there's not much more to tell."

Frankie frowned. "So, who is it? Do I know him?"

"No, I don't think so. I don't even know him."

Frankie looked perplexed and leaned back in her chair. She slipped her phone out from her back pocket and said, "That's fine, what's his name? We can both find out."

Jamie gulped. "No, like, I don't know his name."

At first, Frankie frowned, confusion all over her face, and then she broke into a broad smile. "Are you serious? James! An honest to God one-night stand! That's not like you."

Jamie shrugged. "I was trying something else."

"Is this about Alex?"

Jamie hadn't really thought about it like that. If she was being honest with herself, yes, it probably had a lot to do with Alex. She was angry with him, frustrated with the revelation of his infidelity, and feeling manipulated by his insistence and repetitive texts that *she* was the one in the wrong. So yeah, her decision to sleep with the first man who openly hit on her after they broke up was absolutely fueled by spite. She wasn't exactly proud of the fact, especially now that she was the one sitting on an exam table, facing the consequences, while Alex was off doing who the hell knows.

At that moment, a series of quick raps came from the door. It opened, and then a small brown head popped into the room.

"Frankie, the phone's for you. It's the ear infection from yesterday and he sounds pissed."

With an eye roll, Frankie peeled herself off of the plastic chair and stood. "We can chat about it later," she said to Jamie, who nodded in agreement, relieved that the discussion was in recess. Frankie went to follow the nurse out.

"Oh," she stopped, halfway out the door. "And don't forget to pick up your antibiotics."

She wasn't feeling much better as she drove to the pharmacy. The sharp pain in her temples returned, and the sun's reflection off the road stung her eyes. A foreign heat returned to her forehead and cheeks, accompanied by a fresh wave of fatigue. It wasn't noon yet and she was ready to go back to bed. She flicked her rearview mirror toward her and took a look at her face. Her skin was pale and lifeless, and her hair lay flat against her forehead, limp and frizzy. Her under eyes looked somewhat bruised, the blue-green capillaries visible through the fragile skin. With a lurch, her stomach gurgled forth a bubbling pain, and she felt a sudden bloat grow against the waistband of her leggings. She was going to need a bathroom soon.

Thankfully, the pharmacy wasn't busy. She stood in a short line, and gave her name at the counter. The tech behind the register tapped on the keyboard, and then told Jamie to give them ten minutes. As if on cue, her bowels shifted and audibly gurgled. She needed a bathroom. Frantically scanning the back wall, she found the RESTROOM sign, and made her way across.

As if her body could sense the looming amenities, the approaching safe harbor, the closer she got to the back wall, the harder her guts clenched, wrenching tighter together. Jamie's teeth chattered and she broke into a sweat, praying to not shit right in the middle of the family planning aisle. She felt pressure, and then a warm dampness spread through her crotch. She couldn't tell if she just pissed herself. Tears squeezed out from the corners of her eyes as she reached the bathroom. She pressed her hands against the door.

Please be open, please don't be occupied. If someone's in there I'm absolutely going to shit my pants.

She pushed, and the door gave way.

Her pants were halfway slid down her thighs by the time she opened the first stall door. She slammed the swinging door shut behind her, sat down, and was stricken with one final twisting cramp as she released a violent gush of hot water into the bowl.

Jamie cried out as her body pushed against the pain, working its hardest to empty her completely. She pressed her wet palms against the stall walls for support. She felt so weak, they might have been the only things keeping her upright. While she felt relief, she also felt unparalleled pain, a sharp thread that tugged from deep inside her, pulling her guts downward and out. She grit her teeth to keep from yelling. Her jaw ached with the pressure.

Soon, the cramps receded, and the pressure released. Jamie's hands shook from the adrenaline as she wiped her cheeks, wet with tears. Wisps of hair clung to her forehead, and with a trembling hand she pushed the pieces off of her face. One deep breath. Two. A third. More able to take inventory of her surroundings, she blinked twice and looked down. With horror she realized she had soaked blood through her pad all the way to her underwear and onto her leggings.

"No, no, no, no," she hissed. Jamie started to panic. She had utterly ruined her clothes and had no way to replace them. She frantically searched the bathroom stall for a solution, as if she would find anything more than the roll of toilet paper and the overflowing tampon dispenser attached to the wall. With no other option, she peeled off her leggings, and then the underwear. With a sick splat, she let the underwear hit the linoleum floor. She pulled a handful of the thick, dry toilet paper off the roll and cleaned herself off the best she could. The feel of the paper on her swollen crotch stung. Afterwards, she rolled the sopping pants back up, grateful that they were black, and winced at the cold wetness against her skin.

She turned to flush the contents of the toilet, and immediately recoiled at the sight in the bowl. The water was bright red, but that wasn't all. Floating in the bowl were what looked to Jamie to be thick, viscous plugs of blood clots. They were so dark they could have been black. She watched with unfurling disgust as the mucosal clots swirled around one another in the still water. She no longer thought what was happening was menstrual.

She pressed the lever, and for a moment of pure horror, watched the toilet water and its murky contents swirl, rise, and nearly overflow, until, with a satisfying *shlurrrp*, the water sucked down the drain.

Jamie exited the stall, dropped the clump of red fabric into the garbage can, and washed her trembling hands. Her reflection stared back as she studied herself. *What is happening to you?* She wasn't naturally terribly thin, but she noticed the protuberance of her collarbones poking through the skin of her chest. In any other circumstance she'd at least feel shamefully prideful at the prospect, but now she only felt the underpinnings of dread. Her eyes were bloodshot from the tears. Her hair tangled around her face. She looked ten years older than she did yesterday. *Breathe.* Jamie allowed the cool water to run over the inside of her wrists. Despite her efforts to tamp them down, she felt new questions rising within her.

Over the speakers rang a tinny voice, garbled in the echoes of the small bathroom: "Jamie G., your prescription is ready for pick up. Again, prescription for Jamie G. ready for pick up."

She left the bathroom, snatched the brown bag off the counter, and ran out of the pharmacy.

Jamie took her first antibiotic dose as soon as she got home, and went to run hot water for a bath. She felt grimy and sweaty and sickly. Her skin was oily and cool to the touch, although she felt feverish still, and restless. Peeling off her clothing under the unforgiving fluorescence of her bathroom lights, she deemed her pants a total loss. There was a slick, greasy redness smeared in between Jamie's legs, onto her thighs, and up onto the loose skin beneath her bellybutton. With a tremulous hand, she reached behind her and felt the discharge particularly thick, caking at the cleft of her buttocks, confirming what she had already suspected. At least some of this bleeding was rectal.

Despite her fear, Jamie had no desire to reach out to anyone.

Since coming home, she dodged a text from Frankie: *Hey how you feeling?* And then one from Alex: *I think I saw your boyfriend at the bar last night. Had a hot girl with him.* Her phone buzzed with several missed calls, but Jamie just turned off the device and walked away.

She sunk into the steaming water, relishing the sting on her cool skin. Her skin flashed pink at the temperature, but Jamie only lowered herself more deeply, past her waist, arms, shoulders, and then her throat. As she acclimated to the heat, she watched with detached fascination as the water grew pink. Her skin began to itch.

The amniotic nature of the water lulled Jamie into a state of relaxation, despite the horrors of the morning. As she fought the urge to fall asleep, the itching sting of the hot water pressed into her, and she absentmindedly scratched at her raw skin.

Jamie didn't have a plan. She didn't think she just had a UTI, but what could she suspect? Frankie wouldn't have told her she had an infection if she didn't. Jamie didn't get sick a lot. She only had a primary care physician in the sense that there was a stranger's name printed on her insurance card for paperwork purposes, but she couldn't recall the last time she needed to see him. Once she took herself to urgent care because she thought she broke her ankle (she didn't), but most things she treated with just an over-the-counter painkiller and a heat pack. The truth is, while her mother was alive, Jamie brought her to so many doctors' offices and emergency rooms that Jamie was happy to never see the inside of a hospital again. They saw all the specialists and ran all the tests. Jamie sat, holding her mother's hand procedure after procedure, enduring the too-clean white walls, the nauseating smell of antiseptics, and the same tasteless food. Through it all was the beeping of machinery, the endless noise even during "quiet hours," and the cries of the dementia-riddled patients mere rooms away. And there in the middle of it all was Jamie, stealing away moments to cry in the bathrooms and behind curtains and during anesthesia, and after all that, her mother still died. Jamie avoided hospitals as best as she could.

The thought only occurred to her after scratching the same patch on her arm for several minutes that she might have a rash. She wasn't prone to reactions to any antibiotics, she didn't think, so right now would be an incredibly inconvenient time to suddenly develop one. She didn't want another reason to reach out to Frankie again.

POCKETKNIFE KITTY

The itchiness persisted, and bred pain.

Now irritable, she withdrew her arm from the water, exposing the pink skin to the chill of the bathroom air. What she saw ignited a foreign bewilderment, a confusion. The synapses in her brain fired, but they weren't connecting to any coherent thought. Finally, something registered.

There, mere inches below the crook of her elbow, was a round, raw flash of irritated skin.

A sore.

6.

From: Price, Carrie <carrie_the_one@firstmail.com>
To: Doe, Julie <anon821425@firstmail.com>
Sent: 4 April 2022, 6:55 p.m.
Subject: The Story

We weren't together long when I made the mistake of sending him my uncropped nudes, and I know. I KNOW. I can feel the frantic typing on your end. But I don't need to be told now. It's such a humongous mistake, but at the time I just didn't know any better. I hadn't been with a lot of guys before him and I guess I just really trusted him. And he really liked them, right? So I sent more. They weren't anything major, truly, just a few selfies in my bedroom and one that I set up on a timer. They were cute but nothing you'd be scandalized by.

Anyway, next thing I know I'm getting sent those exact photos by friends of mine, and then by acquaintances, and then by total strangers. A lot of them were just looking out for me, telling me that Ethan had sent them to a bunch of his guy friends and then posted them on a bunch of amateur sites. And just as many of them were from anonymous assholes just looking to brag that they had seen my tits or that they had jacked it to me. I wish I could tell you that I let it roll off my back or that I blocked his number and moved on, but no, I was livid. I was so fucking embarrassed. I called him and texted him, but he just totally ignored me. I tried reporting him, but the cops just sort of blew it off. It was like pulling fucking teeth to even get them to tell him to take down the photos. He said he did, but by then the damage was done. Nothing truly is deleted off the internet, you know? Things just get reposted and reposted, they spread like a disease, and then it becomes impossible to contain. And by that point, I was getting tagged in a new photo on a new site almost every day. My parents were even getting sent them. Do you know how mortifying it is to have your dad tell you he's been getting sent screenshots of your nudes? The man already had one heart attack. He can't take the strain.

I'm really not the violent type, honestly, but I wanted to hurt him so bad. Nobody could help me. Nobody gave a shit.

Carrie

JAMIE HAD NEVER been more grateful to work in her own cubicle. She knew she looked awful. She didn't bother with any make up today. She didn't think there was any use. Both her skin and lips were dry and flaky. Her swollen eyes were viciously bloodshot, but the fragile skin around them tinged a sickly green color. Jamie would have loved to have covered them with a touch of concealer, but she simply didn't have the energy. She came in early to avoid contact with any coworkers and immediately took refuge at her desk, angling her chair so her back was facing the entry. Self-consciously, she patted the back of her head.

Last night, after her bath, her hair started to fall out.

It wasn't a lot at first. She found that when she dried her hair, more strands than usual were simply left behind in her bath towel. And then once she went over with a brush, even more pulled out, tangled in the bristles. Fearful trepidation and sick curiosity soon drove her to run her fingers through her hair, and in the end she wasn't surprised at all to see her hands come away spiderwebbed thickly with loose, wet strands. With no effort, she was able to pull them out of her scalp, painlessly, with her bare fingers. Knowing she should resist, yet unable to, she combed through with her hands, over and over, and watched strings of wet hair fall at her feet sadly and soundlessly.

Jamie spent the rest of the evening sitting on the edge of her bed, wrapped in her towel, with a small rag folded beneath her. She thought of very little.

The sun set outside, and her bedroom gradually darkened in shadow. She wasn't sure how long it took her until her mind slipped away back to that night. It felt like weeks ago. She wrenched her brows tight, eager to recall the details, but the memories slipped through her fingers like a hand through sand.

"What did you give me?"

Jamie saw him in her memory, dark hair and thick brows, light eyes, saw what initially attracted her to him. She remembered his strong hands, deft fingers tracing the rim of his glass. Rubbing his palms together, hearing the sound of skin on skin. Imagining those hands on her. She saw the stubble on his cheek and mildly wondered how the coarse hair would feel under her fingers. She could almost smell the warm musk of tobacco on his cold leather jacket as he inched closer and closer to her. However, the more Jamie saw him in her mind, the clearer he became. Like staring at an optical illusion, she saw the mirage and the truth simultaneously, occupying the same space in her brain. He wasn't as enchanting as she had remembered. He possessed a strong nose, yes, yet it was speckled with unflattering blackheads at the nostrils, and his lips were thinner than she remembered, more chapped at the edges, dry and unwelcoming. She remembered the sex, hasty and desperate, and wondered how it all fit into the puzzle.

She was vulnerable, Jamie recalled. A mere week prior she called it quits with Alex, and then spent that time dodging his hateful messages. She found herself teetering on the edge of two fears: the fear of engaging, and the fear of cutting him off. If she engaged, she'd encourage his relentless chasing. If she cut him off, well, Jamie knew the ways he could retaliate. He knew where she worked. He knew where she lived. No move felt correct. No matter what she did, she'd be saddled with bearing the brunt of whatever consequence he'd dish out to her. It wasn't fair. She was hurt, bitter, and willing to do whatever to move past him, but frozen between two equally shit options. So, in a lame effort to grant her brain some level of reprieve, she ended up in BAR NEON, trying not to stare at her phone, hoping she could delay her choice for one more evening. Jamie wondered how she may have looked to an outsider. Did she stand out in some meaningful way? What about her anxiety-riddled demeanor raised a flag for this guy? Why did he have to pick her?

"Who the hell are you?" she thought, fiddling with the peeling cuticles of her fingernails. Her skin had long since dried from her bath.

He had approached her with almost no hesitation, confidently and assertively. He slid in so easily, ragging on the bar with Jamie, appealing to her sarcasm, and then buying her a drink with a slick slide of a debit card.

With a jolt, Jamie remembered.

She saw a small plastic rectangle. The flash of lime green and orange. And a name.

Stoker.

"As in Bram, right?"

The twist of fate, the moment they chuckled over.

But no. He didn't find it funny. With an adjustment,

she remembered his reaction. The subtle shielding with his hand, the self-conscious deception. He didn't just want to play it sexy. He just didn't want Jamie to know his name. Why?

Slowly, an irrational, desperate idea began to form in Jamie's mind. That desperation was the only reason she agreed to come into work today. She knew she wasn't going to do any actual work. She would wake up early, get dressed, drive to the bank, settle into her cubicle, and prepare to do something entirely illegal.

She was afraid to brush her hair this morning for fear of pulling out another clump, so she gingerly gathered it all at the nape of her neck and tied it loosely with a scrunchie. Her bangs kept falling out of the tie, however, and she eventually gave up trying to contain them. The sad, lank pieces did nothing to combat the sick way she felt, but the energy to care evaded her. If no one came by her desk, she could continue to avoid personal contact, true, but for how long?

As she booted up her computer, Jamie couldn't stop staring at the lesion forming on her arm. It looked similar to a cigarette burn—ovoid in shape, the wound itself open and raw, yellowed on the edges with pus, frantically trying to heal. But unless Jamie was mistaken, the sore only seemed larger today. The skin around the wound was angry, red, and swollen. Against her better judgment, she touched the edge with her finger, felt a sharp pinch of pain, and immediately pulled away.

"Fuck," she hissed. "What the hell did you do to me?"

Renewed bitterness and justified anger bubbling inside her, she logged into their system.

This was so illegal.

She opened their account manager. This program held the records of anyone banking with Sprout Credit Union.

All she knew was a last name. As hard as she wrenched her brows together, she couldn't bring to memory any sense of a first name. Seeing the image of the plastic debit card, turning it over in her head, did nothing to help. She truly had nothing more to go on. Thanking her good luck that he didn't have the last name Smith, she typed STOKER into the row marked LAST NAME and clicked SEARCH. She held her breath as the results loaded.

NAME	SEX	DATE OF BIRTH	ACCOUNT NUMBER
STOKER, ANDREW M.	M	07/14/1995	100103181
STOKER, DYLAN	M	12/02/1987	104252015
STOKER, JESSICA L.	F	04/20/1992	100110510
STOKER, JOHN W	M	9/10/1961	100102406
STOKER, JORDAN	F	08/21/1989	10012256

There were only five results, three of which were men. Running her cursor over the names, Jamie did a couple quick calculations in her head, and could immediately eliminate John. There was no way the guy she met was approaching his sixties. That only left Andrew and Dylan, both men in their twenties to thirties. The Stoker she met truly could be either.

Trying her luck, she clicked on Andrew's account and scrolled through his transaction history. His account seemed typical for a twenty-something: fast food purchases, a gym membership deduction, a direct payroll deposit from a local clothing retailer, but nothing that provided any clues.

She exited and clicked on Dylan. She prayed to no one in particular that she'd find something, anything. His account loaded and with trembling hands, she scrolled. The transaction history looked very similar to Andrew's. There was a streaming service payment, a couple coffee orders, what looked like an electric bill payment, a gas station purchase. And then she saw it, under Recent Activity:

10/16/2021   BAR NEON LLC-$19.12

There it was, their fucking drink order.

"There you are, you bastard," she whispered. She found him. Dylan Stoker. It was all there for her: his phone number, address, his balance, and even his goddamn social security number. She scrolled to the bottom of the page and felt a sharp sense of *schadenfreude* at his embarrassingly low account balance. She tabbed back up to his demographics. The address listed was a P.O. Box, which wasn't very helpful, so the phone number would have to do.

She grabbed her cell phone immediately. If she gave what she was about to do any amount of thought, she would talk herself out of it altogether. She tapped the number on her screen, exhaled between pursed lips, and waited as the phone rang.

Three rings later, the line picked up.

"Hello?" It was him. It was his voice. He spoke in a quiet, careful tone. She wondered if he was at work, puzzling at the unknown number calling him at nine a.m. Jamie was surprised he even answered.

Jamie swallowed. "Is this Dylan?" she asked in a small voice.

"Uh yeah? Who is this?"

Jamie remained silent. She hadn't thought of what she was going to say if she had gotten this far. What was there to say? *Right after fucking you, my body began falling apart like an unspooled rag doll. What do you have to say for yourself?*

The lesion itched horribly.

"Hello?" he repeated. Jamie felt the hesitation in his voice.

Her uncertainty quickly shifted to anger. It bubbled inside her, pressing against her bowels. She felt a violent throb form in the space behind her eye sockets. She wanted to reach through the phone, curl her fingernails through the parting of his lips and tear the thick muscle of his tongue out of his fucking throat.

He was silent. For a second, Jamie thought he was going to hang up, until she heard his stiff reply. "How did you get this number?"

"What did you give me?" she whispered through gritted teeth.

He didn't reply.

"You gave me something. What is this?" Jamie blinked back hot tears.

The line clicked off.

"Hello?" No reply. "Fucker!" she spat. She dialed the number again, but the call was sent to voicemail. She tried once more, and again after a singular ring she was diverted to the mailbox.

"Fuck!" she hissed, ending the call. She considered calling from her office landline, but thought better of it. Blocking every number Jamie tried to call from would be as easy for him as a press of a button, and the attempts wouldn't get her anywhere.

The call sent Jamie's mind spinning.

Dylan Stoker.

He knew something, Jamie was positive. There was *something* to know. And this wasn't just a random one-night stand. A paranoid tingle in the back of Jamie's brain told her this was somehow intentional.

Targeted.

Had he known who she was? If so, how long had he been following her? What did he want with her and what did he know about her illness that she didn't? The sores weren't a coincidence, and neither was the infection, the blood, the hair falling out of her head. Jamie felt a rolling sensation deep in the pit of her stomach, and wondered if there'd be anything more.

With renewed horror, she realized she had been

scratching at the lesion.

She tore her hand away and saw blood under her fingernails. Holding her arm up, the lesion had opened up, raw and bleeding, milky red fluid seeping along her skin and dripping onto her pants. She shot up out of her seat, arm outstretched and away, desperately looking for something to clean herself with. She spotted a tissue box on the other side of her desk, pulled out a few, and pressed them into her skin.

Without logging off her station, she snatched up her coat and her bag, and tore out of the building.

7.

From: Price, Carrie <carrie_the_one@firstmail.com>
To: Doe, Julie <anon821425@firstmail.com>
Sent: 5 April 2022, 1:41 a.m.
Subject: The Story

Anyway, like I said I'm not the violent type, so I really had no idea where to start if I really wanted to get back at him. I'm actually fucking embarrassed to say I started by just Google searching "how to get revenge on an ex." Mostly I got a bunch of elder millennial listicles and a few blogs about getting a "break up body" which were actually just advertisements for weight loss pyramid schemes or crossfit cults or whatever else. Basically they were all lame. I mean, I wanted to hurt him. He ruined me. Like, if anyone ever tried to look me up for a job or something, those pictures wouldn't be hard to find. They could haunt me forever. So no kiddie shit. I was beyond glitter bombs and sugar in the gas tank. So I was looking for next level shit: rip out his car's transmission, kill his fucking dog.

Anyway after a good amount of searching I found myself on reddit. And Jesus there's some dark shit there. I scrolled for hours, subreddit upon subreddit, subreddits about revenge and crime and stories from girls who had been horribly wronged, assaulted, beaten. I got lost in this doom spiral, taking in all this trauma—some of these girls were actual girls, like thirteen- and fourteen-year-olds, all retelling some of the most disgusting things I've ever heard. Cracked out moms selling them out for drugs. Their stepbrothers touching them after the rest of the family had gone to bed.

Carrie

HER BATHROOM WAS the only safe place to be right now.

As soon as she got home from work, fresh cramps hit Jamie, and she only just made it to the toilet in time. However, even after flushing away the evidence, the blood didn't stop coming. She stood, dizzy, staring down at her legs, watching viscous pink fluid running down and puddling on the cold tile floor. Instead of fruitlessly trying to wipe herself clean again, Jamie curled up on her bathmat and let herself fall asleep.

She hadn't left the bathroom since then. She couldn't recall if it had been one day or two.

As the new day's light crept in through the small window above her sink, Jamie thought a lot about her mother. She wondered what her mother had thought about in her final days. With a ping of disgust, Jamie realized she never asked. As much as she was present for appointments and procedures and testing, they never really talked. Jamie didn't know if her mother was scared or ready or relieved. By the time the illness escalated, there wasn't anything left to ask. She had forgotten who Jamie was. She had forgotten who *she* was. Jamie didn't know if her mother was in pain or if the narcotics had properly taken over. She didn't know if her mother understood what was happening to her. Somewhere deep down, did she have the awareness to know she was dying, locked away inside her mind someplace? Or maybe the dementia was merciful, wiping away the truth entirely, stripping what was real from the pulp of her cerebral cortex? The truth is, Jamie's mother scared her. Every time she looked at her mom, weak, frail, shitting into diapers, she was reminded of the inevitability of her death, how close death was to *everyone* she knew. She was reminded of just how out of control she was.

Jamie wondered how long it would take to die, and wished for the ignorance her mother must have felt.

She did consider calling Frankie again. What she was planning on telling her, she didn't know. She knew she couldn't help her. Whatever was coursing through her body wasn't something she was going to be able to diagnose with another urine test. She felt a shifting in her body, an uncanny movement in her gut. She couldn't label it but she knew it was something monstrous, alien. Inhuman.

So instead Jamie lay on the tile, staring into the fluorescent ceiling bulb, and let the bathmat beneath her continue to saturate with whatever was pooling out from her body. With vague interest, she watched as a fly circled the light fixture and bounced rhythmically against the exposed bulb. The pain in her head throbbed with the *buzz* of each contact.

By now, the lesions had grown in number. The skin on her arms and legs were sore with them. There were several on her shins, knees, calves, one more on her arm, and a new one forming in an uncomfortable spot between her shoulder blades. The itch was terrible. As much as she tried to ignore them, she picked. She scratched. She peeled the scabs. Blood flowed onto the tile, but the sight didn't deter Jamie. The original sore, the one from yesterday, was open and deep, revealing pulpy red flesh. The more she scratched, the more agonizing the itch. With particular fervor and irritation at the sensation, Jamie scraped the surface violently with her fingernails, crying out as to why the hell this was happening to her, when she felt a new sensation. A sharp pop.

With detached curiosity, she looked down.

Two of her fingernails had come loose off the flesh of her fingers, popping like hinges off a rusty screen door. There was no blood yet, but the sting of pain hit mere seconds after Jamie saw what she had done. She sat up and looked at her hand, unsure what to do. With the fingers of her other hand, she gently squeezed down on one of the nails, pressing it back onto the raw nail bed. She winced through the pain that shot up her forearm. She released the nail, and to Jamie's lack of surprise, it gently hinged back up again.

She spun in place, twisting herself around to reach the cabinet under the sink. She pried open the door and fumbled for her meager first aid kit. With trembling hands, she found a small package of adhesive bandages, unwrapped a few, and weakly reattached the fingernails to their respective swollen fingers.

It was then that there was a knock on the front door.

The sound was a shock to her nervous system, rooting her in reality, reminding her she still lived in this world. In this world, people went to work. People ordered take out. People paid their water bills. They knocked on doors. People were going about their lives with absolutely no knowledge or awareness that just mere houses down, a common banking representative was transforming into what Jamie could only describe as a monster.

The knock came again. This time, she could also hear a voice.

Jamie crawled to the door of her bathroom and craned her neck out. She was afraid to track blood on the hall carpet. Her mother agonized over choosing the pile. If Jamie listened carefully, she could make out what was being said.

"Jamie, come on, don't be like this."

Alex.

How many days had it been since she spoke with him? She was starting to lose track. How long had she been in the bathroom?

Knock, knock, knock. "Jamie, I see your car in the driveway, I know you're home, okay? Look, I know I've been an asshole. I just want to talk."

Jamie shifted her weight from one knee to the next and waited. A jolt of memory tingled down her spine. She didn't lock the door when she came home. She hoped he wouldn't try the handle.

"Jamie." Knock knock knock. "I know you can hear me. Listen," he paused, "I broke up with Liz, okay? We're done. I know I did you dirty. Jamie, I really don't want to do it like this, one of your old neighbors is gonna call the cops on me or something."

Jamie licked her lips. They were dry with dehydration; she didn't remember the last time she had any water.

"Jamie, I've been texting and calling you."

Had he? Jamie realized that she didn't know where her phone was. She scanned the bathroom, but the phone was nowhere. Where did she have it last? She thought back to yesterday—she was pretty sure it was yesterday—as she ran home from work, the urge to shit twisting her stomach into sweat-inducing cramps. Bursting in the front door, throwing off her coat, sprinting through the kitchen, toward the bathroom, and—

—tossing her bag on the floor in front of the hall closet.

Jamie whipped her head around the corner, and there it was. Her purse, thrown haphazardly, innards spilling out onto the carpet.

"I just miss you, Jamie. I really want to come in so we can talk."

Jamie stood, careful not to slip, as the majority of the bathroom floor was coated in a thin red slick. Crouching for stability, she inched toward the linen closet. Grateful that she did her laundry recently, she pulled out a clean towel, clutched it to her chest, and turned back to the bathroom door. She stood on the tile, toes carefully tucked behind the carpet boundary. A fleeting vision of her as an Olympic diver sprang to Jamie's mind. She unfolded the towel.

Alex was still talking at the door, but she had stopped listening.

Jamie wafted the towel down onto the carpet like she was making the bed, doing her best to line up the edge within arm's reach of her fallen bag. She hoped to crawl along it like a bridge and reach out for the strap of her purse. If she was careful, she could avoid ruining her mom's carpet. Towel in place, Jamie carefully bent to her knees and began to crawl. Her palms and knees left bloody imprints on the cream cloth as she moved. She felt one of the sores on her right knee open against the fabric and she grimaced.

The tips of her fingers reached the end of the towel. The bag still looked too far away. She stretched her arm out, but only felt air. She lowered her body to the towel, pressed against the ground with her toes, and tried again. She felt a muscle pull someplace deep in her side, but pushed through. With a grunt and forward thrust, she was able to stretch out just enough to feel her fingers wrap around the purse strap.

She dragged the bag toward her, dug inside, and withdrew her phone.

She didn't hear Alex anymore. At some point he must have given up and left.

Luckily the phone still had some charge. She tapped on the screen to unlock it, but the phone wouldn't respond to her bandaged fingers. She shifted the phone and tried her left hand, but her fingers were imprecise and sloppy with fatigue and weakness, and so, frustrated, she tore the bandages away with her teeth. The effort pulled the dangling fingernails right off with them.

Jamie gasped in pain and stared down at her hand. The first two fingers of her right hand were completely devoid of their nails. The newly exposed skin was red, raw, and beginning to swell. They looked alien, and she immediately thought of E.T.'s finger with the glowing tip. They throbbed as Jamie stared. She fought the sick instinct to put them in her mouth. Instead, she turned her attention back to her phone. Fingers freed, the screen began to respond. Jamie tap tap tapped with thick, pulpy fingertips.

Missed calls from work. From Frankie. From Alex. Voicemails. Texts. She dismissed them all. She had just as many junk emails clogging her inbox. Scrolling through the notifications, she felt a sharp gurgle in her bowels.

She stood on weak legs and moved to the toilet.

And then stopped.

Jamie's mind couldn't immediately process the new sensation. She stood, mid-stride, toes flexing against the bloody tiles beneath her, and touched her hand to her stomach. It wasn't an urge to use the toilet she felt.

It was movement.

She felt a shifting of weight, deep where her bowels were. Where they should be? Even medically illiterate, Jamie sensed inherently that everything inside of her was moving. Her stuff—her guts . . . everything she was made of, hung low in her abdomen like overripe fruit . . . she sensed it settling lower in her gut than where it should be. Waiting. But for what? An answer came to Jamie, and she thought it before she could censor herself.

To fall out.

As soon as she thought it, she felt the shifting travel from her bellybutton to her groin. She had been consistently bleeding for days, but this felt different. She looked down at herself. She expected to see her belly distended, swollen, but it looked the same as it always had. Her legs were smeared red still, caked with drying blood and pockmarked with the sores she'd grown in the past couple of days. As horrific as she appeared, she looked no different from the outside. Curious, Jamie stuck two fingers into the waistband of her underwear, long since cold and saturated with blood and unmentionable fluids, and wondered why she bothered to keep them on at all. If not for the sake of social norms and the taboo of nakedness, Jamie contemplated, she would have thrown them out the day before. Continuing to wear them gave Jamie at least the illusion of security. Cautiously, she pulled the fabric out and away from her body and peered within.

At first, she didn't know what she was seeing.

It looked like she was peeling apart the guts of a used tissue. She pulled the fabric away from her body, and saw her underwear was full of thick, stringy pus, like colorless snot. Through the mucus she could see her flesh and the multiple excoriated lesions pockmarking its surface. She wondered how many of the sores were *inside* her.

Electricity shot up Jamie's spine. She felt dizzy. Disoriented. The odor was overwhelming. It was sweet, pungent. Rotten. The smell turned her stomach.

She didn't want to touch. She knew it was bad.

In that moment, irrationally, Jamie's mother's face swam in her vision. Her eyes were lucid, wise, completely unlike the waxy glaze Jamie had seen far too many times. Her eyes were alive. Without hearing a word, Jamie knew the eyes were saying: *Get that bastard*.

Jamie folded down onto the wet tile and supported herself on her hands and knees. Her vision swirled. She couldn't remember the last time she ate. Her stomach clenched with the reflex to vomit. The hideous odor lingered in her nostrils and she gagged against the thick air, but nothing came up. Her stomach was completely empty. Sweat beaded on her forehead and she wiped it away. With effort, Jamie regarded her phone and pulled up her contacts. She clenched her jaw, gnawing her lips. Tasting blood. As she chewed her own mouth, she felt her teeth move ever so slightly against the pressure. She knew better, but she pressed her tongue against them, a compulsion, and resisted the urge to keep fiddling.

Those will be the next to go, she thought with disinterest.

Hands trembling, she tapped her phone awake and searched. Her fingers, lazy and error prone, kept pressing the wrong buttons. Her blinks grew longer and heavier. Fatigue was creeping up quickly, and the threat of unconsciousness was a warm blanket. It was a race to the finish line before she succumbed to sleep. Finally, she found what she was looking for, and she typed.

Her message to Frankie was brief: *I need you to find Dylan Stoker.*

8.

From: Price, Carrie <carrie_the_one@firstmail.com>
To: Doe, Julie <anon821425@firstmail.com>
Sent: 5 April 2022, 12:25 p.m.
Subject: The Story

I eventually found myself on r/nuclearrevenge when deep in the subreddit I came across an unusual post for the page. Someone with a clearly anonymous username and a blank profile pic simply posted a link labeled "try this." Nothing else. It didn't have any upvotes and it didn't have any comments. I wasn't so sure about it at first, it could have been a virus. But on that particular night, I had a few glasses of wine in me so my attitude towards most things were very "fuck it." I hovered my cursor over it just waiting for a sign, and then clicked.

Carrie

BY THE TIME Jamie woke again, she had missed a dozen texts and phone calls from Frankie. She scrolled down her phone, now smeared with blood that she had long since stopped trying to wipe clean, and read:

James where have you been I've been texting you
Are you okay?

Who the hell is dylan stoker??
??????
I swear to god I'm this close to calling the police

Jamie rolled onto her back and stared into the ceiling light once more. The tooth she felt moving against her tongue was much looser today. She pressed her tongue against it and felt it give easily, felt a pulling sensation deep within her gum tissue. She reached a finger inside her mouth and hooked it around the tooth. Exerting very little pressure, she pushed inward, and the tooth came loose. A quick spurt of warm liquid hit the back of Jamie's tongue, but she didn't feel much pain. She pulled it out and examined it very briefly before letting it fall onto the bathroom tile and roll away, never to be seen again.

Jamie once read something about a phenomenon called terminal lucidity, where a dying person who was otherwise confused experiences sudden mental clarity prior to the moment of their death. During this time, the person can regain formerly lost functioning like walking and talking. They can experience an increase in energy, and by all accounts can appear to suddenly "get better." Scientists haven't been able to agree on what exactly causes this or why, but it's a phenomenon that's been observed in many dying people. This lucidity, sometimes called the *rally*, can give unsuspecting families unwarranted hope that their loved one has made a miraculous recovery. There are tears and prayers and phone calls to relatives. However, days, or even mere hours later, death occurs. The rally is named as such due to the appearance of the patient's final "hurrah," their enthusiastic *rally* in the face of their demise.

Jamie's thoughts were foggy and disorganized. She felt no such burst of energy or rush of cognition. She wasn't thinking clearly. Her concept of time was slipping through the cracks of her mind. She found herself closing her eyes and reopening them, unaware if five seconds had passed, or five hours. Chuckling dryly, Jamie felt reassurance. Death must be further away than it felt.

Jamie's mother never appeared to have had a rally of her own. At least she never had the walking, talking, laughing kind of rally Jamie read about. Jamie never felt a surge of hope or a compulsion to thank the heavens for the blessings of the miracle given to her mother. In her final days, Jamie's mother remained glass eyed, nonverbal, and utterly out of touch, up until her organs quit and her heart stopped and the social worker walked in with the stacks of paperwork.

However, Jamie couldn't help but wonder if, even for the briefest of moments, her mother experienced a silent rally. Maybe she felt an inner lucidity, an awareness that no one could see or sense, and that in those moments she knew exactly who she was, where she was, and what was happening to her. If that was the case, she wondered if her mother ever prayed for death.

The lesion on Jamie's arm, the first one, was open again. It itched horribly, so she just continued to scratch it. By now the skin of her forearm was open like wet tissue paper. One of her fingers that still had a nail was nestled inside, buried up to the first knuckle, scratching sweet relief. Jamie knew it should be painful, peeling back the thin skin like opening a birthday gift, but she really felt nothing. She marveled at the vague numbness of it all.

Next to her, her phone began to ring. In her periphery, she could see the name of the caller, bold, in all caps: FRANKIE. With slippery fingers, Jamie picked it up.

"Frank?"

Frankie's reply was immediate and frantic. "Jamie? Oh my God where have you been? Are you okay? Jesus, I've been trying to get a hold of you for days, no one's heard from you."

Jamie didn't know what to answer first. While she processed Frankie's line of questioning, Frankie pushed on.

"What's going on? Where are you?"

"I'm home."

"Are you sick? What's wrong? I can barely hear you."

Jamie pushed herself up to a sitting position and heard the sick peeling sound of her skin pulling off of the sticky tile. "Um," she considered both of her palms, and chose the cleanest one to rub her eyes with, "yeah I'm pretty sick."

"What's wrong?"

What *was* wrong? Jamie rolled over a series of overlapping thoughts in her brain, weighing the success each would have if introduced. *My hair's falling out. I'm peeling my fingernails off like scabs. I keep forgetting where I am. There's some mystery snotty fluid oozing out from my vagina and my asshole. My teeth are falling out. I'm covered in hideous, painful open sores. I'm sitting in a pile of blood in my bathroom, I don't know how long I've been here, and I don't know if I'll ever leave this room.* She lost her nerve, and simply replied, "I'm not sure."

"Do you need an ambulance?"

"No." Despite her state, Jamie still insisted she avoid the hospitals. She wasn't dumb. She knew her ragged, failing body wasn't something the understaffed and underfunded local emergency room was equipped to handle. Something more sinister was happening, and at least one person out there had answers. Somebody knew exactly what was happening to her, which is why she wanted Frankie to help her find Dylan.

"Did you get my text?" Jamie asked.

"Yeah." Jamie could hear the frown in Frankie's voice. "I did. Who the hell is Dylan Stoker and why do you need to find him?"

Jamie considered where to start, but anything she could have said would sound crazy. So instead she said nothing. She told Frankie she could explain in person, that she wouldn't believe her until she saw with her own eyes. That she needed her help. She told Frankie it was okay to come over if she promised not to call an ambulance. Frankie agreed and hung up.

Jamie's eyelids felt thick again. Her vision blurred. She

tried to blink away the exhaustion, tried to force her eyes more awake, but her body felt so heavy. Her eyes ached. The blackness of the back of her eyelids felt like a warm embrace, and Jamie was so cold. She would shut her eyes for just a moment, she decided, and hopefully when she opened them, she would have a fraction of her energy back. No sooner had her lids closed that she was awakened by a series of heavy knocks on her front door. She was immediately fuzzy and disoriented. She wasn't sure how much time had passed.

Jamie heard the front door open, followed by a jangling of keys and quick footsteps.

"James. Jamie? Where are you?"

There was no need to direct her movements, as mere seconds later, Frankie appeared in the doorway of the bathroom.

Jamie didn't need to imagine how the scene looked. She knew it was horrifying. The bathroom was an assault to the senses. Snotty red fluid smeared along the bathroom floor, up onto the walls, into the bathtub. In the sink. On the door. Everywhere Jamie had touched was defiled, tainted with the thick, brazen, red filth. The smell must have been overwhelming for Frankie. And in the middle there lie Jamie, a mass of bloody sores, lying in a puddle of her own blood and fluids. A crown of fallen hair rested like a halo around her head. Irrationally, Jamie felt embarrassed by her lack of pants. She looked up at her friend. The horror was all over Frankie's face. She stared down at Jamie and gripped onto the door frame.

"What the fuck happened to you?"

Jamie sat up. "It's a lot to explain."

"Who did this?"

The true answer was complicated. Jamie replied with a simple, "Nobody."

"It looks like a goddamn crime scene in here." Frankie clasped a hand to her open mouth, eyes wide, taking in as much as she could. She thrust her hand into her back pocket and pulled out her phone.

"What are you doing?"

"I'm calling an ambulance."

"Don't you fucking dare," Jamie growled.

Frankie stopped, eyes wide.

"A hospital can't help me."

"The fuck it can't, look at you."

"No," Jamie said. "Something else is happening here. Something worse."

"Your *arm*, Jamie!"

"Will you just stop and listen?"

Frankie did.

"I just," Jamie began. She measured her words before she said them. Frankie was beyond disturbed. She didn't have any warning of what she was about to walk into, and Jamie did that to her. "I need you to just listen to me. If after I'm done, you want to leave and not be a part of any of this, you can. But I just need you to listen. I need you to be my friend. Can you do that for me?"

At first, Jamie wasn't sure that Frankie would even stick around long enough to hear the end of her sentence. Frankie did stick around, however, and then in response did absolutely nothing. She said nothing. She moved no muscle. Seconds passed. Jamie, eager to fill the silence, bit back the urge to keep talking. She waited her friend out, lungs burning from the breath she was holding. Frankie's face fixed in a frown, eyes hovering someplace on the wall behind Jamie. Jamie didn't know what Frankie was doing, but she definitely knew she wasn't turning away and walking out the door. Finally, with a shaky exhale, Frankie slid her phone back in her pocket and toed off her sneakers. She entered the bathroom and, doing her best to sidestep the blood spatter, slowly approached Jamie. She did so cautiously, like she would a wild animal. Jamie sat still, doing her best not to alarm her friend. Frankie stopped once the blood made it impossible to move any closer, and knelt down in front of Jamie.

"James. You need to tell me what's going on here."

So she did. Jamie started at BAR NEON. She told Frankie the story of how she met Dylan, how he came onto her. How she flirted back. How they came back to her place. She told her about the weird sex. About Alex's visit. Then the blood. The sickness, and how it spread. The fingernails. The hair. The phone call. Through the explanation, Frankie did as Jamie asked. She remained silent. She listened.

"Do you have any idea what they'd do to me if I showed up at a hospital somewhere? Do *you* think they'd send me home with an antibiotic? Do you think they'd send me home at all?" Jamie reasoned. "You don't think there'd be some hush hush phone call placed to like, I don't know, the CDC or the Governor or something? You don't think there's some protocol for medical mysteries like this? And if they suspect that it *is* contagious?" She could hear her voice sound slightly unhinged, the paranoia rising with her pitch.

Frankie appeared to ponder this. She repositioned into a crouch in front of Jamie, balancing on the balls of her feet. She rested her elbows on her knees, steepled her fingers against her closed lips, and looked carefully at the scene around her. Jamie considered that after all this, Frankie still would decide that Jamie needed an emergency room, or even worse, a psychiatric unit, and that she'd be on her phone calling for EMS within seconds. Frankie would decide that Jamie had, in fact, snapped under the grief of her dead mother and the messy narcissistic abuse of Alex, and that she'd hurt herself. She'd caused the sores and she'd starved herself, and blamed the entire thing on some mystical sexual encounter she had on a wild impulse. If Frankie believed that, there wasn't much Jamie could do except relent. Jamie waited patiently for her fate.

Finally, Frankie spoke.

"So how do we find this guy?"

Frankie helped Jamie clean up. She did the best she could to wipe up the floor, the walls, the tub. Jamie sat plaintively in the far corner of her bathroom, knees tucked under chin, trying her best not to get in the way. She watched as Frankie poured capfuls of bleach onto the tile, alternating a filthy sopping red rag with a dryer, pink tinted one, scrubbing her hands raw with each swipe. She ran the tub full of water and used it to rinse off the places she had cleaned. After the floor was wiped, Frankie cleaned the tub and then refilled it with clean, warm water. She carefully helped Jamie undress, and then helped her into the bath.

As Frankie and Jamie worked together to wash away the blood, to clean her skin, and carefully rinse out her fragile hair, they discussed. Frankie was always much better at tracking people's online movements than Jamie ever was. In most cases, if someone had a public social network profile and used their true name for the page, Jamie had no problem searching and finding them. However, things got difficult when people weren't as public, or when they used a fake name, or when they never posted.

Frankie never let any of that stop her.

Once, back in college, Frankie got rear ended by a stranger in a little white Chevy. The guy instantly drove off, but not before she jotted down his license plate number. Her car didn't sustain much damage, but rather than just letting the issue go, she used the license plate to link it to the vehicle registration through some shady online database, giving her a first and last name.

Searching that name didn't result in any active social media accounts.

So instead, she found his tax records, and thereby his W-2s, and tracked down where he worked. That company had an active social media presence, and after a brief scroll through one of their accounts, found a MEET THE TEAM post, where she was able to put a face to the name. When she eventually cornered him outside his office building,

Frankie threatened to call the police and charge him with no less than three separate misdemeanors. Thoroughly flustered and doing his best to prevent a scene in front of his coworkers, the guy offered to pay for Frankie's car repairs completely out of pocket, so long as she swore to leave him alone.

"All I need is to be able to find him. To track him to a public place."

"And then what?"

Jamie shrugged. "I don't really know, but I have to do something. I need to know what he knows."

The pair planned for hours, only stopping once in order for Frankie to leave for the pharmacy and return with a roll of gauze and a tube of thick ointment. She cleaned Jamie's wounds the best she could and wrapped the injuries. Jamie's skin was dry and clean, and once all the blood was wiped away, she felt halfway human again. Afterward, Frankie made a salty, protein rich soup. Jamie was clearly dehydrated, and Frankie all but forced the spoon down Jamie's throat. Even though Jamie had lost a lot of hair, there was still enough to tie back. Frankie gently towel dried the hair, combed it, gathered it with a loose elastic, and let it fall down Jamie's back. Jamie sat on her bed, wearing her shirt from Welcome Week, and turned in Frankie's direction as she spoke.

"And what if he doesn't tell you anything?"

Jamie knew what would happen.

9.

From: Price, Carrie <carrie_the_one@firstmail.com>
To: Doe, Julie <anon821425@firstmail.com>
Sent: 6 April 2022, 5:13 p.m.
Subject: This is where shit gets good

So the website, right? At first I thought the link was broken. For a few moments nothing loaded. My screen was totally black, except for my cursor hovering stupidly in one of the corners. Then I realized that the link had taken me to a website. I found the scrollbar and dragged until I got to text. There was a large, plain text header that read:

Catalogue: Retribution Rituals for the Divine

Beneath that were dozens of hyperlinks that when opened led to more hyperlinks. Some links were dead, many weren't even in English. I clicked and clicked, deeper and deeper down the rabbit hole, until I found a working link. It led me to a page with the header:

Invoking the Spirit: For Urgent Action Against a Wrongdoer

It was as if the page had been specially suited to me. The writer described that the actions to be spoken of should be reserved for perpetrators of sexual crimes, and that through this, they would face the ultimate punishment. As I scrolled, half drunk on cheap boxed wine, I let the fantasy carry me away. I remember thinking that there's no way this was real, but whoever wrote out these instructions sure did seem to believe it was.

I don't remember everything I was supposed to do, and I don't plan on trying to seek the page out again. I don't think I have any business messing around with that shit anymore, considering, you know, what's happened.

Carrie

THE NEW DAY'S sun came through her bedroom window as Jamie quietly woke. Or something resembling waking. She wouldn't call the groggy etherized fog she floated through all night sleeping. As the moon reached its peak in the sky, Jamie lay suspended in a state of half-twilight sleep, watching the passing car headlights flicker against her bedroom walls, and then disappear into nothingness. She felt this midnight haze once before, right after her mother's death. She had trouble sleeping, so she took an over-the-counter sleep aid, and spent the night half awake, half dreaming, and wholly anxious, simultaneously aware and yet not aware of the room surrounding her. With lids ever so slightly open and heart rate noticeably above resting, Jamie felt very much aware of the aching, the itchiness of her skin. She lay on her mattress like a living corpse, and soon felt a slithering sickness deep in her bowels. She looked down at her stomach. Her belly was full with an unnatural roundness. The mound pulsed like a heartbeat. Like it was alive. Jamie felt paralyzed; her arms were too heavy to move, so there they remained, stupidly by her sides. She watched the pulse grow in intensity, but she felt no fear. She felt nothing at all. With a sharp tug from behind her belly button, she watched her stomach bulge up and out, beyond the capacity of normal human stretch, and split wide open like a burst balloon.

It was starting to be difficult discerning what was real and what wasn't.

The morning sun was bright and crisp, and she was so tired. She put a hand to her belly, but of course it was intact. She squinted into the fine rays of sun streaming in from her window. The brightness distorted her vision. She rubbed the sleep from her eyes, but the blurriness persisted. She rubbed again, pressing a little harder into her skull, but it didn't seem to help. Jamie blinked twice, and took turns winking each of her eyes, assessing the vision in both. She seemed to see okay out of her left eye, but her right eye's vision was clouded over. She held up a hand, closed her left eye, and sure enough the skin of her palm lacked any definition. She only saw a vague, flesh colored shape.

Nothing was in her eye at all. Her vision was simply failing.

Last night after cleaning up, Frankie propped Jamie up in her bed with a shrug, and told her she would check on her. She plugged in Jamie's phone to its charger and rested it on the mattress next to her.

"I'll check in tomorrow night after the clinic and change your bandages. Call me if something bad happens," she said.

"Something bad. Right."

Both Jamie's arms and legs were covered in white gauzy bandages, giving her an almost comedic cartoon mummy-like appearance. She could bend her arms, but only barely. The dressings seemed to provide her flesh the support it needed, but not long after Frankie left, Jamie noticed blossoming red stains forming through the gauze.

She didn't know how long she'd have before the bandages would be soaked through. She wondered how long it'd take for her bedding to suffer the same fate.

During her bath last evening, Jamie made a horrifying discovery. As she carefully washed between her legs, wincing against the pain of the raw soreness of her skin, she watched the water in the bath grow pinker and pinker. It was disgusting, yes, but also strangely satisfying. As one cleans, the other dirties, like a cycle. Like it was always meant to be. Jamie's fingers gently scrubbed her skin, scratching away the caked-on blood and gore from her thighs and pubic hair, and once those were clean, she moved her hand up her leg to her sensitive center. No sooner had her fingers made contact with where her labia should be that she was met with a sickening bony protuberance at her fingertips. It was an immediately alien feeling, nothing like the soft fleshiness she'd felt there all her life. With a frantic gasp, she pulled her hand away, splashing pink water onto the bathroom floor. From her angle, reclined in the bath, she could see nothing between her legs. Hesitantly, she gathered the courage, arched forward, and craned her neck downward to look. Now that so much blood had been cleaned away, she could finally see herself. The skin had denuded away, and what was left behind was slick and shiny, flesh that was pulled taut like a painter's canvas. The skin wasn't alive. It resembled dull scar tissue. It was a garish, pinkish green color, with remnants of the yellowed pus she had been washing away. In the middle of all the rotten skin was one large hole, gaping, like a screaming mouth, as if it had eaten away at itself. Desperation and nausea clutched at her gut, and though all instincts screamed at her to pull back, she couldn't look away. She kept staring, expecting to see something emerge from the black hole she had grown. A live birth. She felt, perhaps, fond of it? Maybe something was living in there, digesting her, and if she looked long enough, she'd catch a glimpse.

Just as Jamie's finger was brushing the entrance to the

hole, Frankie entered the bathroom and, horrified, dove her hand into the murky water to yank Jamie's hand away.

The best Frankie could do was stuff an incontinence pad into Jamie's underwear and hope it'd hold back most of the snotty red flow. To be safe, she folded all the clean towels in Jamie's linen closet into a neat crosshatch pattern on top of her mattress, and set Jamie atop. They hoped it'd be enough for now.

A rhythmic buzzing next to Jamie's ear pulled her back to the present. She picked up the phone and squinted at the screen. An incoming call. Her boss's name flashed on the screen.

The day she ran out of the bank, she dodged about four phone calls from him, and then ignored the three during the next day. He hadn't called back since. Jamie, of course, wasn't too bothered over this; she had been doing all she could to keep her body intact. But why was he calling now? She nearly dismissed the call, but some tugging deep below her belly button told her to pick up, to at least explain her absence, even if the damage was already done.

She swiped to accept the call and cleared her throat.

"Bill, hey, listen—"

"I figured you'd answer if you thought it was Bill calling."

The voice didn't belong to her boss. It was a familiar voice, but Jamie's brain couldn't process the information quickly enough.

"I'm sorry, what?" With effort, she pushed herself up onto her elbows, balancing her phone between her ear and shoulder.

"You've been avoiding me."

Everything clicked into place. The voice finally registered.

"Alex?"

"I told you to answer my calls," he said, speaking in a low, quiet tone. His voice felt close to the receiver. It crackled slightly with static. The sound tickled her ear.

"Alex, what the hell are you doing?"

"Your car has been at your mom's house for days, so I know you've been home."

Jamie pulled back her phone to examine her screen again. Sure enough, Bill's office number was listed on the incoming caller ID. Confusion fogged through Jamie's brain, pieces of a puzzle crumbling in front of her eyes.

"Alex, Jesus, why are you calling from Bill's phone?"

"Oh," Alex replied in a cold tone, a smile in his voice. "We're just having a meeting. I took the opportunity while he stepped out to give you a ring. I had a feeling you'd be more likely to pick up if it was him calling."

"Why are you meeting with my boss?"

"Well, you see, there's been an investigation. It's a pretty big deal around here."

Jamie's head began to pound, her vision swimming. She pressed the heel of one of her palms into her good eye. "Alex, can you please just tell me what the fuck you're talking about?"

"There seems to have been some illicit activity within the branch, you see. Fraudulent transfers, account activity in some pretty high-profile accounts. Activity that looks like it leads back to your computer. Your log in."

"That doesn't make any sense, I haven't been to work in days. I've been sick. I haven't been a part of any transfers at all," Jamie said, annoyed that she had to explain herself at all to Alex.

"Not according to your computer."

Her brain felt anesthetized. Her tongue, thick. None of this made sense. She hadn't been to work in days. And the fact that Alex was somehow wrapped up in things, somehow involved, sitting in Bill's office, the disconnect picked at her like a healing scab.

Then it hit her.

Reality settled into the gaps, it clicked together in one horrific motion. It was only in that exact moment that Jamie realized what Alex was getting at.

Tuesday morning. Logging in. Calling Dylan. And then never logging out.

"Alex, what did you do?"

"And me," he continued, his tone paradoxically light and conversational, "I was so worried. I hadn't heard from you, so I took it upon myself to reach out to your boss. Maybe he's seen you? But he seemed downright devastated. See, he hadn't been able to get a hold of you either. And then there was this talk of an anonymous complaint, a major client missing a whole lot of money. What a disaster."

"Did you go to my work? Did you get on my computer?"

He ignored her. "So I told him that you've definitely been home, and that, now that he mentioned it, you've been having some money problems since your mom's death. She left you with nothing and the funeral expenses were more than you were planning for."

"Alex, for fuck's sake! Were you in my office Tuesday?" Spit flew from her mouth. Bile rose in her throat, but she was stuck. Trapped in her house, captive by her own body. She could do nothing.

Alex's voice changed, low and threatening, "Now you listen to me, you stupid bitch. No one rejects me. No one humiliates me. And no one ignores me. This is the least of what's coming to you, do you understand me? I know where you live, I know where you work, I know your feminazi carpet munching best friend and I've been to the office she works at."

Jamie's skull prickled at the mention of Frankie.

"You don't think I could meet her there one day? You don't think I know which one her car is? You don't think I couldn't do something to her?" As he spoke, his voice rose in pitch, feverish. Excited.

"Alex," Jamie began, "I don't know what you're thinking but you need to—"

He rolled right over her words, as though she had never spoken them. "I could destroy everything you care about. You think some work mishap is the worst I could do? I could ruin your whole fucking life, Jamie. I—" Then a pause. A brief shuffling.

The phone hung up very suddenly.

With fumbling fingers Jamie tried to redial the line, but was met with a dial tone.

She tried to push herself up and out of bed, but as soon as she was righted, she was met with an overwhelming sense of nausea. Hot stinging bile splashing against the back of her throat, and she clamped a bandaged hand to her mouth, but the vomit spilled out between her fingers like ribbons and splashed onto her lap. The sick bitter odor hit her nostrils, triggering a violent throb in the space behind her eyes. Jamie bent over, pressing her palms deep into her closed eyes. She imagined pushing so deep into her sockets that the jelly in her eyes compressed and burst, flooding her skull with the warm liquid, and maybe at least for a second, providing relief from the pain she felt. But there was no relief.

Jamie cried out into the empty room, screaming for help that no one could provide.

The day pressed on, and soon the evening sun splayed hot orange across the foot of Jamie's bed. She had resolved to lie back in bed and wait for Frankie's call. She tried to crawl to the front door, to do *something*, but no sooner had Jamie reached her bedroom door that logic settled in. Even if she got to her car, she was too weak to drive. The most she'd accomplish would be freezing to death, halfway loaded into her driver's seat, stuck, naked toes blackening with the sunset.

Here in bed, Jamie's feet felt warm beneath the glow of the sun, and it was so nice to feel just one pleasant thing. October was drawing to a close and the sun was gone from the sky by 6:30 most nights. She presumed it was about that time. Jamie was just about to give into the warm, welcoming draw of sleep once more when the phone in her hand buzzed.

Not eager to receive another hateful call from Alex, Jamie lifted the phone to her face with the intention of turning it off altogether. However, right before her finger made contact with the button, Jamie realized it wasn't Alex at all. It was Frankie.

The text was brief: *I found him.*

10.

From: Price, Carrie <carrie_the_one@firstmail.com>
To: Doe, Julie <anon821425@firstmail.com>
Sent: 7 April 2022, 12:07 a.m.
Subject: TMI but you asked

To start, I had to collect some things. Some stuff was easier to get a hold of than others. I needed to collect drops of my own menstrual blood, which was just as exciting as it sounds. I also needed his DNA. The instructions didn't specify. It could be whatever I could get my hands on: semen, blood, hair, saliva. That was a hard one. I hadn't seen him in weeks so I didn't have anything. It's not important to the story how I got it, but trust me when I say it was gross. Some things were a little easier. I needed a bunch of herbs and spices and oils and very specific candles that I could only find online. Some things I already had: a mirror, a pot to boil things in, a knife. It took me a few weeks to collect everything, especially since I had to wait for my period to come first.

The instructions referred to it as a Curse of Fornication. I had to follow very precise directions. Once the moon was at a specific lunar phase, I had to combine the items in a very particular way and recite a whole bunch of words in a language I didn't understand. After that, I had to fast for three days. I could only drink water. That was the worst part. The fasting was supposed to make me more spiritually attuned by weakening my physical body. I'm not sure it did all that, but it did give me a terrible migraine and made me a bitch to everyone I knew. And then, according to the page, after the ritual was complete, I would have to fuck him. I wasn't leaping out of my seat at that step, but according to the directions, it was the final instruction, the one that would set the whole ritual in motion. Afterward, it'd pass to him. And then once passed, it would start working. See, it was supposed to create an illness, a rotting sickness that would eat at him from the inside out, infect him and kill him in the most sickening way. Organ prolapse, skin decay. Real sick stuff, we're talking the indie horror paperback shit you get from a pal at school and hide from your mother. To be honest with you, I didn't really believe in it. I don't think you'll believe me, but it's true. Either way I sure as hell was going to give it a try. What was the worst that could happen? I didn't care if he died.

So the sex part, that actually wasn't very hard. He was more than willing to come over if he thought it meant him getting laid. He wasn't suspicious at all, and why would he be? He was an idiot. So that's exactly what I did. I burned the incense and lit the candle and hid the herb concoction under the bed and said the words and slid the mirror under the pillow and smeared my blood on my inner thighs and I texted him and he came over. And it felt right. It felt good. I knew it worked.

I can't explain it, but I knew I did it.

Carrie

THIRTY MINUTES LATER Frankie was hoisting Jamie up to her feet and helping into a pair of socks and slides.

"He posted about NEON less than an hour ago and all of his replies say he's still there," she explained, with more excitement in her voice than Jamie would have expected. "The evening is early and who knows if he's the bar hopping type. If we hurry, we should be able to catch him."

"I knew I could rely on you," Jamie said slowly and carefully. By now several of Jamie's teeth were loose in their sockets. They shifted uncomfortably with any excessive tongue movements. This made basic speech very difficult. She tried to speak as little as possible.

"You know me, I could track a Mennonite through their social media presence," Frankie said, grinning.

"I didn't think Mennonites had—?"

Frankie smirked and rolled her eyes.

"Oh, yeah I get it."

Frankie rambled on for a few minutes about Dylan's posts, speculating on who he might be with, where he was, and for how long he might be there. She calculated the odds of finding parking on a Saturday night, and wondered aloud if she had quarters for meter parking. She spoke conversationally, but with some restraint, and Jamie wondered if Frankie was actually enjoying herself.

"If I had thought about it before I left work, I'd have made sure to grab a handful from my desk just in case. You don't happen to have any—"

"Hey Frank," Jamie interrupted, "do you think I could have a mirror?"

Frankie stopped, and after a moment of hesitation said, "I don't know if that's a good idea."

"I haven't seen myself in days. If I'm going out in public, I want to know what I look like."

Frankie crossed her arms over her chest and although she seemed to consider this, she didn't respond.

Jamie touched her cheek with her bandaged finger and, sighing, reasoned, "Listen, someone's gonna call the cops or an ambulance or something if I look like I just crawled out of a morgue so can you just do what I'm asking, please?"

Frankie chewed on her bottom lip, considering, and then turned to the dresser on the far side of the bedroom. Jamie kept her makeup and skincare products there in a series of disorganized piles, along with whatever clothes she had worn and deemed too dirty to rehang, yet too clean to throw in the dirty clothes basket. Frankie opened the top drawer, rifled around the mess for a second, and then withdrew a circular hand mirror.

"View at your own risk," she sighed, tossing the mirror onto the mattress. It landed mirror-side down and made a soft *phlump* a foot away from Jamie's legs.

Jamie reached for the mirror and wrapped her fingers around the cool plastic handle. However, instead of turning it over, she laid it on her lap and rubbed at the smooth back with her thumbs. She knew it would be bad. The last time she looked in a mirror was in the bathroom pharmacy. How long ago had that been? Four days? Five? It felt like weeks ago.

"If you're gonna look, look," Frankie said, leaning against the open doorway. She shoved her hands in her pockets. "Time's a-wastin', James."

Jamie flipped the mirror over and stared into the reflection.

With a shudder, she nearly dropped the mirror. Her stomach turned, nauseous, and her pulse quickened. There was no other word for it, she looked terrifying.

The flesh of her face had become flat and rubbery, seemingly devoid of any ability to emote or contort. There was no color in her cheeks or her lips, except for the sores. Two sores had formed on her neck, and a third was bubbling to the surface at one of her temples. Jamie's eyes were two large silver dollars in her skull, and the fragile skin of her under eyes sagged with a sickly green tone, making her gaze appear lost and forlorn. Jamie's right eye was milky, opaque with vision loss. She had lost a visible amount of hair. She could clearly see the silhouette of her scalp through the dry tangles. The remaining hair was thin and fraying at her crown and temples. Her lips cracked at the edges and the blood that seeped from the slices smeared across her mouth, giving her the garish look of a circus clown gone mad. She bared her teeth and looked in her mouth. Two of her teeth were missing, one a molar, not very visible, but the other, an incisor, was impossible to miss. She couldn't remember when she had lost that one. Her gums had receded with dehydration and decay, and the remaining teeth looked overlarge, horse like, in her mouth. Her tongue was covered in a thick white film that she itched to scrape off.

"Here," Frankie said, tossing Jamie a gray hoodie from her closet. "Just," she made a gesture akin to pulling the drawstrings tight.

Jamie pulled it over her head, tucked her hair into the hood, and did as instructed.

"Better?"

"Better."

Frankie wrapped Jamie's arm around her shoulder and helped walk with her to the front door. "God, you reek," she groaned.

They made their way through the house and down to Frankie's car. She helped load Jamie into the backseat with a grunt, settled into the driver's seat, and then started the engine.

"What are you going to say to him if you find him?"

Jamie pretended not to hear, and Frankie didn't ask again.

The drive was short. Jamie leaned close to the window and watched her town roll past. Jamie remembered one of the last times she had driven her mother to the emergency room. She and Frankie nearly mirrored one another, except Jamie was the one driving, and it was her mother who was slumped across the backseat. It was dark out, chilly, and Jamie chanced repeated glances over her shoulder as her mother vomited down her front. She did her best to monitor her mother and encourage her to lean forward so she wouldn't choke, because they couldn't afford an ambulance. As Jamie rode the waves of nausea, she wondered if her mother was ever as scared as she was at that moment. The window fogged with each of Jamie's exhaled breaths, and she watched as the street signs, corner lights, gas stations, and pedestrians faded away behind the haze.

A few minutes later, Frankie reversed into a parallel park along the street, and through the window, Jamie heard the pulsing bassline, muffled, as though underwater. A couple of people walked past the car, and Jamie shrunk farther into the fabric of the seat. Frankie pivoted around, arm resting on the back of the passenger's side seat. She looked at Jamie.

"Let's go."

They exited the car, Frankie assisting Jamie where she felt weak, but actually Jamie moved relatively well. Something about the proximity of the bar, Jamie thought, gave her some renewed energy. She absorbed it, the sounds, the odor of alcohol that seeped onto the street outside. Near the entrance, three girls stood with warm jackets wrapped around their torsos, wearing glittery miniskirts, pale legs bare to the cold. One of them clenched a cigarette, talking at the others, while her friends nodded to the music and tapped on their phone screens. The glow from their screens underlit them, casting shadows that reminded Jamie of summer camp urban legends. Flashlights as microphones. Wet summer youth. Heat, sunburnt skin. Being fingered in the dark behind the cabins. Jamie felt powerful as she watched them. Their youth radiated off of them like a stench. And although she only wore dark leggings, a pair of rubbery house slides, her old Welcome Week tee, and a threadbare hoodie, she felt protected. Her over large tee shirt hung down past the hem of her hoodie, and she gripped the loose fabric. It felt like armor in her palms. With a nod to Frankie, she rubbed away any lingering blood on her lips with the raw cotton fabric of her sleeve and pulled the drawstring tighter so that only her eyes, nose, and lips were visible.

There was no ID check at the door, of course. No velvet rope. Just a small door with a small plastic sign in the window: BE PREPARED TO SHOW ID. NO ONE UNDER 21 WILL BE SERVED.

They entered BAR NEON and were instantly swallowed by the vibrating bass and the pulsing purple lights. Jamie followed closely behind Frankie, head lowered as much as she was able, fearful of recognition. Jamie imagined a nightmare scenario: a passing twenty-something, beautiful, with thick and flowing caramel hair, approaching too closely, making eye contact. With a look of disgust and perhaps a quivering pointer finger, she withdraws into the crowd. Screaming about the monster in their midst. Soon, sirens. An investigation. Arrest, taking Jamie someplace hidden and not exactly legal. Then doctors, studies, experimentation. She felt the fear of the sterile hospital walls, the solid cot and the scratch of dry linens on her palms. But Jamie quickly realized she was completely invisible. No one looked her way.

Jamie observed the club from behind Frankie's shoulder. She felt like she was seeing with new eyes. She remembered a mere week ago what it was like for her, sitting at the bar and passing the same blanket judgment over the other patrons. Contempt rippled in her guts. She felt better than them, but she was never better than them. She looked into their round faces, slick with sweat, and where she once saw resignation, she now saw desperation. Desperation to be seen, loved, chosen. Jamie saw nervous hands pulling self-consciously at garments, tucking bangs behind ears, sucking in stomachs. Pick me. Choose me.

Like lambs offering sacrifice, they displayed their bodies for one another. Jamie remembered feeling so vulnerable. It was no surprise she was picked off like a scab.

Frankie leaned in close. Her breath tickled Jamie's ear. "Do you see him anywhere?"

Jamie squinted into the room. Her vision wasn't as strong as it was a few days ago, and the dim lighting and flashing neon made it more difficult to discern details around her. She shook her head.

"Should we split up?"

Jamie wondered the same. She felt steady enough to move around the club, and knew that they would cover twice as much ground if they split, doubling their chances of finding Dylan before he left.

"Yes," Jamie nodded. "You take the far left wall by the bar and I'll hang over here and check the bathrooms. We'll meet back here in ten, okay?"

"Are you gonna be okay?"

Jamie nodded. "Go. I'll see you in ten."

Frankie stepped away and was swallowed by the crowd. Jamie dodged an incoming barrage of drunk twenty-something men and narrowly avoided getting beer spilled down her back. She shuffled her way to the closest wall and tried to maintain a steady grid pattern with her eyes. Across the back wall, down the first row of tables, loop back in an oval, back to the bathrooms, repeat. From her angle, she could see Frankie sitting at the far corner of the bar, armed with the photographic memory of Dylan's profile picture.

Jamie's bowels shifted, and she felt a sharp cramp.

Fuck, not here.

She shoved a fist into her stomach, kneading against the pressure. She couldn't afford an emergency now. The knot in her stomach radiated, and pain pressed into her lower back, curling around her spine. The nerves braided through her vertebrae sizzled with pain. Small beads of perspiration formed along the perimeter of her forehead and were immediately absorbed by the taut cotton pulled over her face. Wetness spread in the seat of her pants and she clenched her knees shamefully. She pressed a pair of bandaged fingers to the fabric of her pants and they came back an oily red. She moved towards the alcove housing the bathrooms and hoped Frankie would be able to find him on her own.

Then suddenly, she saw him. About fifteen feet away, Dylan Stoker, smiling widely to a small group. He drank a beer and clapped another man on the back while the rest of the group roared with laughter. He bobbed his head to the music and observed the room around him passively. His fingers tapped on the glass of his drink like an afterthought. Jamie remembered those fingers, those hands on her. The thought made her physically ill. Jamie didn't move, fearful that any perceived motion would signal her presence, and send him running like a spooked deer. But she was so close. Now that she saw him, he seemed to glow in the club lighting. The shine of his teeth, the neat trim of his beard. She could almost feel him at her fingertips. Why couldn't he feel her?

Jamie chanced a look at Frankie, still at the bar, wondering if she noticed him. That way, the two of them could triangulate and maneuver him into a controlled position, and Jamie could try to get answers out of him. Frankie, however, stared out in the opposite direction. She didn't see him. There wasn't any way to signal her. Jamie's eyes flicked back to Dylan, and a snap of electricity clapped at the base of her skull.

He was looking directly at her.

For an agonizing several seconds, the two of them stood like opposing statues as the purple neon danced across their bodies. Dylan's jaw locked tight and his eyes were wide and anxious, fearful even. None of his friends seemed to notice. Jamie felt like Tony and Maria in the West Side gymnasium, two breathless people sharing a private connection in an oblivious crowd, detached from reality for the smallest moment. Except in this reality, Jamie wasn't falling in love.

She wanted him dead.

Without preamble, he turned and fled in the opposite direction. Completely abandoning the bloody emergency tearing into her stomach, Jamie quickly followed behind. Dylan wasn't running, but he moved with purpose, dodging people, elbowing past thick crowds, making haste. He was headed, Jamie realized, to the rear wall, to the glowing EXIT sign at the ceiling. Jamie hurried and closed the distance. She shoved through a small group, eliciting a few "*What the hell?*"s, but she didn't stop. Jamie kept her eyes trained on Dylan's head, on the V-shaped patch of dark hair that trailed down the back of his neck. He reached the back wall and turned the corner, nearly at the emergency exit. Jamie was only an arm's length away. She thought she was going to lose him altogether until Dylan glanced over his shoulder to look behind, and his feet tripped himself up. As he turned, Jamie was able to reach out, grab the shoulder of his jacket with a clenched fist, spin him, and lead him around the back corner, out of sight from most of the crowd. He dropped his beer and it crashed on the linoleum below. With a greater force than intended, Jamie shoved him against the wall with a grunt.

"What did you do to me?" she cried through gritted teeth. She knotted the fabric of his clothing tight in her fists and pressed, pinning him to the wall.

"It's you" he gasped, eyes wide, clawing at her hands. His eyes frantically searched Jamie's face.

"Tell me what you gave me."

"You called me," he said, shaking his head, as though he could undo the truth by denying its existence.

"Tell me," Jamie growled. As she grimaced, she felt the cracks in her lips reopen. Warm blood oozed down her chin.

"Oh shit, it worked," he said, a mixture of disgust and awe smeared on his face. He continued to try to wriggle away, knees knocking into Jamie's thighs. His eyes darted back and forth, as if hoping to catch the eye of an approaching patron or bartender.

"What worked? What is this?" Jamie demanded. Spit flew from between her teeth. She tightened her grip on his clothing.

Dylan shook his head desperately. "I don't know what it is."

"You're lying," she snapped. She could feel her throat tighten as she asked, "Why? Why me?" She felt water on her cheeks and, with detached awareness, realized that she had begun to cry.

He said nothing. Behind them, hot electronic music pumped through the sound system, and the floor vibrated under their feet.

"Did you know me? Did you choose me? What did I do wrong?"

"No," Dylan said, shaking his head. His forehead glistened with sweat. She felt the panic radiate off of him. "I didn't know you; it was random, I swear."

"So you're here, going to give it to someone else then, huh? Some poor unsuspecting girl just throwing herself at you? Is she next?"

"What? No, it doesn't work like that."

"Work like *what*?" Jamie begged. She knew he knew something. She'd pry it out of him if it meant bending back his fingers one by one until they snapped.

"I—I don't have it anymore," he gasped.

Her heart leapt. The implication that he had it at one point and was cured, the possibility that she could be fixed, desperation hung on every part of her. She stared wildly into his eyes. His jacket shook in her fists.

"What?" she said.

"I don't have it, you do. You have to pass it."

That wasn't the response she expected. She faltered for a second.

"Pass it?"

"That's all I know, I swear. Pass it. The way we did. That's what you have to do."

The way we did. Jamie pulled back slightly, her grasp slackening on his shirt.

"I don't know what you're—"

"That's what you have to do," he repeated. Sensing her hesitation, he slipped out of her hands. With a small glance of pity in her direction, he slid past her and ran for the door. The door slammed shut behind him. Jamie never saw him again.

11.

From: Price, Carrie <carrie_the_one@firstmail.com>
To: Doe, Julie <anon821425@firstmail.com>
Sent: 8 April 2022, 3:00 a.m.
Subject: (no subject)

The thing is, I did something wrong. I must have. I don't know what happened, but it didn't work the way it should have. Weeks later I saw him at the grocery store, completely fine. Just totally healthy. He looked normal. I didn't get it. He was supposed to be a bag of rotting meat by now, but here he was, squeezing avocados for ripeness in the produce section. But he had a girl with him. And her color looked off.

Carrie

AFTER DYLAN RAN out of the emergency exit, Jamie shuffled wordlessly back toward the front of the bar, swimming through the damp bodies. The main space was now flooded with a pulsing strobe light, giving the crowd a static, alien-like appearance as they thrashed to the booming music. The sound hit her ears, but it echoed muted and distant, as though she were hearing it from the bottom of a pool. Suddenly she felt claustrophobic. Her armpits were moist and they chafed as she moved. She untied the drawstring knotted beneath her chin, loosened the taut fabric, and allowed the hood of her sweater to fall from her face. The dampness of her skin and hair cooled against the bar air, and she inhaled the odor of hops.

Frankie appeared to Jamie's right and held tight under her arm. She leaned in close. Her mouth moved, but Jamie couldn't make out what she was saying. Jamie shook her head vaguely and floated to the exit. Frankie came alongside.

The drive back to her house was a mostly silent one. Frankie saw Dylan run out the back exit of the bar, and then intervened on Jamie as she approached the front. Frankie tried futilely to get Jamie to tell her what happened between her and Dylan, but Jamie was tired of talking. She had exerted a lot of energy on Dylan. By now the vision was completely gone from her right eye, and she couldn't tell if it was just due to the volume inside BAR NEON, but she felt as though her hearing was starting to go, too. Everything sounded muffled. Sounds became indistinguishable from one another, blurring into a cacophony of static as it hit Jamie's ears. In the backseat, she hung her head and stared down at her hands. Her bandaged hands were red with seeping blood, the effort of restraining Dylan reopening the wounds beneath the gauze. Frankie motioned to Jamie's hands and her lips moved: *I'll fix that.*

Back at Jamie's home, Frankie helped her out of her soiled pants and into fresh ones. She offered to take a look between Jamie's legs but Jamie waved her off.

"Gyno isn't your specialty, remember?" Jamie said with a dry smile.

Frankie removed the bandages from Jamie's hands and arms, revealing raw decay. Her skin gleaned with the wetness of an unhealed wound. And God, it stung in the open air. The papery skin hung loosely, near rotten, off the bone. With a gasp, Frankie fumbled for a fresh roll of gauze, but Jamie pushed her hands away. Her bones felt heavy with fatigue. She rubbed the fragile skin of her under eyes, and Jamie inhaled the stench of liquor, sticky on her skin.

Jamie lied to Frankie about what happened with Dylan. She told her that he didn't know anything and that he said he'd call the cops if she contacted him again. The lie just slipped out of her mouth. She wasn't entirely sure why she didn't tell Frankie the confusing truth. Maybe fiction was easier to believe. Frankie believed what Jamie told her, and then once again brought up the topic of a hospital. In response, Jamie asked Frankie to leave.

"If you want to check in with me tomorrow, you can. Leave the door unlocked so you can get back in. But for now, I need to go to sleep," she said.

Frankie did as Jamie asked. Jamie didn't feel confident that she wasn't going to wake up to an ambulance siren in the morning, and so she contemplated this being her last night in her mother's home. She sat cross legged in the middle of her bedspread and smoothed the wrinkles in her comforter. As she sat, she thought about Dylan.

He was so afraid as he stared back at Jamie, pinned against the back wall of the bar. She could still feel how he resisted her, how he clawed helplessly at her hands, eyes bulging in his face. Jamie marveled at how both of her interactions with Dylan perfectly mirrored one another. She experienced him in the waves of mid-orgasm, and then in the paralyzing fear of a man cornered in the dark. Both equally vulnerable, exposed. She felt an emotion rise in her chest, but couldn't quite name it.

So what are you gonna do?

Jamie heard the echoes of her own voice in her head. She knew she only had a few options. She could continue to sit on her bed and wait for an ambulance. She could call Frankie back and they could call together, and whatever fate awaiting her at the nearest government medical facility would just be. It may be the last place she'd ever visit, but at least she would be there when answers emerged. Jamie considered her body. She could, she thought, just end it all right now. She still had a jumbo bottle of Tylenol in her bathroom and if she could keep the pills down long enough without vomiting, she could be dead by morning.

Or, the voice whispered, *there's a third option.*

Jamie considered the fact that Dylan could be telling the truth. Some twisted part of her believed him. The possibility that whatever was coursing its way through her veins was sexually transmissible seemed fantastical, but at this point Jamie was willing to believe anything. Was it so unbelievable that there existed a virus that rapidly broke down human tissue to the point that it rendered its host incapacitated before they knew they were infected? It wouldn't be the first of its kind. She recalled word of mouth diseases of childhood lore: necrotizing fasciitis, gangrene, compartment syndrome, hemorrhagic fevers, parasites. Kids would crowd around a computer screen and search for images of the foulest diseases imaginable and play a game of chicken for who could sustain the gore longer than the rest. When she died, would her parts end up on the other end of a search engine, just waiting for a group of preteens to use them in their after school antics?

She thought about the sex again.

Could it really be that simple?

Simple. Jamie scoffed loudly into the silent room. She regarded her rotting body. The flesh of her arms was soft and hung heavily off her bones. She was afraid if she pressed too hard, her finger would push through, like puncturing the rind of a rotten pumpkin. That caused considerable complications if she hoped someone would volunteer to fuck her, and that wasn't even to mention her teeth, her hair, or the odor emanating from between her legs.

The darkness swallowed Jamie as she sat on her bed. She said nothing, just listened to what her body was telling her. She closed her eyes and felt the pulsing pain behind them, the scratching at the jelly of her eyes that no amount of a pharmacy painkiller could touch. The aching in her shoulders, radiating down her spine and crunching into her lower back. Every movement was painful. She felt the deep rumbling, shifting soup of her bowels, but nothing would pass. Her stomach was totally empty. Once in a while a sick burp would escape her lips, and she would taste rancid, sour bile in the air. She was acutely aware of the growing hole at her center. Jamie had initially wondered if the hole was waiting to birth something into the world, but now she wondered if it was waiting to swallow something else up entirely.

There was movement in the bedroom doorway, and Jamie flicked her eyes toward the darkness. There in the opening she could determine something, a defined mass, pitch black and humanoid in shape. Through her clouded vision she could make out no discerning face and she had no sense of relative height or weight. It said nothing and did nothing, but Jamie knew. She knew it was her mother. She felt a tightness in her chest and a thick mucus rising in her throat.

"Mom?"

Silence answered her.

Jamie couldn't be certain if what was happening was real or not. She continued to stare at the space in her doorway, refusing to blink, afraid that if she did, the shape would disappear entirely. Her eyes stung as she stared.

"I'm sorry, mom," Jamie sputtered, suddenly between tears.

The shape didn't move.

"You scared me for so long and I resented you. I didn't want to take care of you, it wasn't fair," Jamie gasped for breath, afraid she would vomit. "You were dying and all I could think about was me. My twenties, lost to caregiving."

The shape continued to watch her.

"I didn't want this." She picked at her remaining nails, peeling them off like strips of wet paper. "I didn't want to come back here after college. But I felt like I had to. What choice did I have? I felt trapped," she said, bitterly. The honesty was good, but the ugly truth heightened her nausea.

"I don't know what I wished I had done differently. Should we have hired someone? Should I have placed you somewhere? I know how hard you fought me on that, but at a certain point you weren't fighting anymore. Maybe I—" she inhaled sharply to catch her breath. "Maybe I should have just taken you somewhere, I don't know." She shook her head and wiped her face. "I did my best, I thought."

The figure remained in the doorway.

"Look at me," Jamie said, pitifully, "I'm going to die and I have no one. I don't have you and I wish I did. God, Mom, I miss you so much."

Her words dissolved into an unintelligible stream of blubbers and sobs as she doubled over, clenching her sides. Snot dripped down onto her cracked lips as she wept but she did nothing to wipe it away. She felt disgusted with herself, with the apathy she felt toward her mother in her final months, that she wanted to wear the ugliness on her skin forever.

Jamie felt a wave of anger coming from the shape of her mother, but it wasn't anger directed at Jamie. It was a bitterness, a rolling wave of injustice and spitting ire. The air was thick with it. Jamie felt it roll across her rotten skin.

Jamie implicitly understood. She felt what her mother felt, absorbed the emotions into her own skin, and, too, felt the cold, detached inequity of her circumstances. Her memories resurfaced the image of Dylan, cowering, mere inches from her face, and suddenly the word for how she felt bubbled to the top: *powerful*. She was a victim, too, God damn it, and if it was the last thing she'd ever do, she would make sure she received justice. She felt in the darkness for her phone, tapped the screen to life, and texted.

Come over.

The shape was gone, if it ever was there.

12.

From: Price, Carrie <carrie_the_one@firstmail.com>
To: Doe, Julie <anon821425@firstmail.com>
Sent: 8 April 2022, 7:20 p.m.
Subject: (no subject)

It didn't take long to figure out what was going on. It was being passed along, like a stolen nude, one hand into the next. Fuck someone and it's gone, out of your system and into the other person. Maybe before you even knew you were getting sick. But what could I do about it? The instructions didn't say anything about that. There was no reversal, no failsafe, no contact information. And it's not like I was going to talk to Ethan about it, what could I say and who would believe me? So I kept quiet. Tried to observe the bar scene. I tried to follow it around the best I could, but I lost it after only a couple exchanges. It became hard to piece people together, keeping track of suspicious looking bruises and thinning hairlines, and if it passed before any physical symptoms developed, it was simply impossible.

So I lost track. I figured I would never find out where it spread. Eventually some poor sap would find themselves stuck at the end, alone, unaware of what was happening to them, and unable to pass it. Their body would end up being studied at a teaching hospital, maybe, I don't know. I watch a lot of sci-fi and read weird shit in books so that's always running through my head. I'll tell you, though, I never anticipated someone in the chain finding me.

Carrie

It was maybe an hour later when she heard the front door creak open. Jamie's heart pounded with fear and adrenaline, but she did everything she could to sit calmly on the bed and wait. She heard the front door close, and then a long pause. No footsteps, no jingling of keys. Just uncertainty and hesitation.

Good.

"I'm in here," she called.

She heard footsteps approaching through the living room, the kitchen, down the hall, and finally ending in her open doorway. A shape appeared, familiar and disproportionately self-assured.

"I thought you'd be mad," Alex mused. He leaned against the door frame, hands shoved into the pockets of his jeans.

The lights in her room were off, and the cloudy skies outside obscured what little moonlight would have shone in through the window. The lone streetlight outside barely cut through the darkness. Even so, she could make out the line of Alex's body, the expression on his face. Jamie sat serenely, cross legged, in the middle of her mattress. She had removed her bandages and taken off her clothes. Her skin ached and the lesions oozed and her teeth wiggled in her mouth, but Jamie was unafraid.

"I'm not mad."

"You're not?"

Jamie shook her head. "I know why you did what you did."

Alex scoffed. "Yeah, why's that?"

"You miss me," she said plainly. "And I miss you. I've missed you, Alex."

Alex wrinkled his brow and glanced, cautiously it appeared, into the dark corners of Jamie's bedroom. His eyes read fearful, as though he were seeing the space for the first time, or prepping for an ambush. "You have?" he said, dubiously.

"Talking on the phone with you made things clear. You aren't ready to let me go. And I can see why. I'm not ready to let you go, either."

Once confident that he and Jamie were truly alone, Alex turned back to Jamie. He wrung his hands together and then rubbed his palms on his jeans.

"It's fucking dark in here," he said, voice wobbling slightly.

Jamie did not reply. She remained seated, legs neatly crossed in front of her, hands gently resting on both knees. The flesh on her chest and thighs goosepimpled in the cool bedroom air. One of the lesions on Jamie's back popped open and she felt warm fluid trickle down her spine.

"What about your job?" he asked.

"What about it?" Jamie shrugged. "I hate that fucking job. Honestly, you kind of did me a favor. I've been looking for a chance to get out for months. You know that."

Alex scoffed. "Yeah, right."

"I'm serious."

"You really expect me to believe that you aren't mad at all?" he said, voice thick with scorn. "And you want to, what, make amends? You want a peace offering? You know how fucking psycho you look, sitting alone in the dark like this? It wouldn't take much for—"

"Alex, I want you to look at me," Jamie interrupted.

He sniffed and crossed his arms over his chest. Leaning slightly closer, he squinted into the dark, brows knitted. Jamie patiently waited as his eyes focused into the darkness. They settled on her body, and the sudden stiffness in the silhouette of his shoulders signaled to Jamie that he saw what she wanted him to see.

"Are you naked?"

"Come here," Jamie purred.

Alex appeared to consider this. If he was smart, Jamie mused, he would harbor some amount of healthy suspicion. If he was smart, he would apply basic reasoning and logic into this bizarre interaction. He would determine that none of Jamie's attitudes toward him over the past week implied any continued sexual attraction and that none of his behaviors warranted such. If he was smart, he'd see the billowing red flags, turn, retreat down the hall, and leave out the front door. But he wasn't smart.

He was an absolute fucking idiot.

"You mean it?" he said. Through the darkness Jamie could see the grin on his face.

Jamie nodded with just enough theater that Alex could see it in the blackness. She curled her pointer finger in a come here gesture and patted the bed next to her. Alex removed his sneakers and shrugged off his coat like shed skin. He approached the bedside table and reached to turn on the lamp.

"No, leave them off."

He paused, then obediently withdrew his arm.

The darkness was her friend tonight. It enveloped her, kept her safe and hidden away. The night felt like velvet on her rancid skin, soothing it in a way she had never known. It would be her protector and her shield. Here in the darkness she was just like any other woman, whole and unbroken. Desirable. Sexual. She could be whatever she wanted to be.

"Come here," Jamie repeated.

He stepped toward the edge of the mattress, and Jamie pushed herself up on her knees. Numb fingers reached for his belt, fumbling with the chunky buckle. The metal clinked under the touch of her swollen fingertips, still aching from the loss of her nails. By this point they were all gone, scattered like breadcrumbs in the woods. At this distance, her and Alex's faces were only inches apart, and she could see the wiry texture of his beard. If she stuck her tongue out, she could probably taste it. As he exhaled, Jamie smelled beer and vinegar.

Alex put his mouth to hers, but Jamie turned away, not wanting his lips to touch her split, scabbed mouth, afraid he would sense the wrongness in her. She pulled the leather strap free from the buckle, and as she did, Alex pressed his face more firmly into Jamie's. He grabbed her by the sides of her face and forced her mouth to his. As he did, Jamie felt one of her teeth near the front of her jaw rip free from its socket. A gush of warm coppery wetness hit the back of her throat and she began to cough. Still, Alex held her to him. Mouths pressed tightly together. All Jamie could do was allow the tooth to slide down the back of her throat.

Jamie forced his zipper down and motioned for him to pull off his shirt. He yanked the fabric up and over his head. Jamie put her hand down the front of his pants and felt him, still soft, in his underwear. As she did this, Alex put his hands on her.

Nothing about Alex's body appealed to Jamie in any way. The things about him that once turned her on now sickened her. She recoiled at the feel of his hands exploring her skin. Up her sides, around her shoulders, down her breasts. That fact that he had spent months touching her body, exploring her with his lips, fucking her, yet didn't seem to notice how wrong she felt in this moment wasn't lost on Jamie. Or maybe he did. Maybe he felt the sores, the slack skin, the gauzy hair. Maybe he just didn't care.

Still, despite her physical revulsion and the sickening disdain she felt for Alex, a deep aching began to build deep between her legs. For all of his best efforts, tonguing the peaks of her nipples and massaging the flesh of her thighs, it wasn't for him that the ache spread. Instead, Jamie felt an energy from outside herself, circling, felt it absorb into her skin. She felt her pores expand and contract, pulling into themselves the heat of the room, the inky blackness that pressed against the walls, and something else. Something she couldn't name. She was breathless with excitement. Something was happening to her, and Alex was somehow completely unaware of it. She squeezed her thighs together and a shock of electricity dashed up her spine. She didn't even know if she technically had a clit anymore. The last time Jamie tried to look, the thick, red, snotty ooze had returned. It stuck to her legs in strings.

Mistaking Jamie's arousal as a personal encouragement, Alex trailed two of his fingers down her belly, over her pubic bone, and in between her thighs.

Fingers sinking into the thick funk, Alex groaned. "Oh fuck, you're wet for me."

The gaping hole between her legs had started to seep again, its raw edges sore and purulent. She could smell herself. She didn't care if Alex did. She wasn't going to need him very long.

Jamie took him by the shoulders and urged him back onto the bed.

"Take off your pants," she commanded.

Jamie sat back on her heels, palms gently resting on her knees. She watched Alex fumble gracelessly with the stiff fabric of his denim pants, pulling each leg off at the ankle. He buzzed with an embarrassing amount of fervor. There was no shame in his childlike enthusiasm and it amused Jamie. As she watched Alex settle back onto the mattress, nude except for the socks, Jamie once more became overwhelmed with feelings of supreme power. The acid burning in her veins was unlike anything she'd ever felt before. She closed her eyes and inhaled the musk of the room, the scent of her. She arched her back and rolled her head gently from shoulder to shoulder and then back around.

When she opened her eyes, Alex's fist was curled around the thick patch of hair between his legs and he held himself in his hand.

"I'm ready for you," he said.

With no intention to play into any concept of foreplay, Jamie climbed on top of him. Alex reached for her, to pull her close, but Jamie simply straddled Alex's thighs and spread open her legs. Although the space between her thighs had become what others could consider alien and terrifying, Jamie now felt something resembling pride in her new body. Her body deserved pleasure and deserved to be seen and deserved the revenge it was going to get. It longed to be filled and she longed to be reborn. She lowered herself onto him, and as he filled her, Jamie was overcome with a raw, animalistic hunger. Something perverse and primal overtook her, something she didn't quite understand, but something she felt nourished by. She didn't grasp what was happening to her, but she submitted to the electricity, the static she felt at the base of her skull and the tips of her fingers.

Jamie moved against him, quickly, forcefully, pulling his body into hers with little regard for his pleasure. She held tight her knees to his waist and pressed hard her palms into his chest, keeping him in place against the pillow.

She paid no attention to him at all. She didn't pay mind to his initial eager gasps, and then continued to pay no mind when his face screwed up into confusion and worry as he watched Jamie atop of him. Jamie was numbly aware of how she must appear to him: frantic, wild, unhinged. She grunted foreign, animal sounds with each thrust of her hips, and cared not one bit for how her body looked to him.

In their relationship, Jamie routinely took care to only have sex in specific positions, to be seen from certain angles only. From behind, from above. She was rarely on top. In her mind the repeated mantra echoed: *suck in your tummy, watch the double chin, pull your hair back*. Even at her most sexual, the ingrained hate toward her perfectly fine body would scratch at her and steal moments away from her. But now, at her most foul and sick, she refused to allow a second more of her life to be sucked from her, to not enjoy what her body could give her. So she allowed her breasts to swing, her stomach to hang, and her face to contort into whatever unflattering expression it chose.

Alex did nothing to further her pleasure. Jamie honestly didn't care what he was doing. As she moved against him, it wasn't his body that sparked the swelling ache inside her at all. She found herself led by something else, something older than the earth itself. It was as if the universe had expanded upon itself in that moment, as if every planet and star aligned in an ancient destiny, as if it was how they were always meant to align.

"Please, please, please," she whispered, head thrown back, longing for the guidance of something unseen, but certainly not unfelt.

Jamie was never religious, not even as a child, but in this moment, she felt the unfolding of centuries' worth of spirituality opening inside her. She was so grateful. She knew that it worked. Tears dripped down her cheeks as she came, crying a feral scream of unintelligible words, doing her best to mirror the rush of orgasm in her skin.

It was done.

Jamie slid off of Alex and rolled onto her back. Alex lay statue still, breathing slowly and silently next to her. Something inside Jamie shifted, and as she lay opposite Alex, naked breasts heaving into the cool bedroom air, she knew it was over. Her body remained broken, but Jamie knew it was only temporary. She would never be broken again. There would never again be fear. It was impossible for there to ever be anything again but peace. She laughed into the quiet room, and tears continued to roll down the sides of her face. Jamie felt the eyes of all the women who had come before her, watching her, nodding their approval. *Yes*, they said to her, *our daughter*. It was amazing that Alex couldn't feel them, too.

She turned her head to him, and through the darkness he met her gaze. His brows were wrenched together, fearful, confused. She could feel his eagerness to get as far away from Jamie as possible. She sensed something grab hold of him from the inside, something new and starving. He couldn't tell yet, but he would. Jamie knew more about him in that very moment than he would ever know about himself. Breathless, she spoke the last thing she'd ever say to him.

"Now get out."

13.

From: Price, Carrie <carrie_the_one@firstmail.com>
To: Doe, Julie <anon821425@firstmail.com>
Sent: 9 April 2022, 10:10 p.m.
Subject: (no subject)

I honestly have no idea what I think is going to happen. It can't go on forever, that's for sure. People aren't sick long enough for the chain to carry on too much longer. From what I've seen, illness comes on pretty quickly, but things start pretty innocuously. A fever, some gastrointestinal distress. Fatigue. It's all seemingly harmless in the beginning. But soon things just . . . aren't anymore. Depending on the person, they can be totally incapacitated within a week. Some people get a few extra days, I guess. Ultimately it looks like if they don't track down the person who gave it to them or figure out what's going on in another way, they're a goner. So I expect it'll die off with someone eventually, and probably soon. I mean by the sounds of it you came pretty close right?

I'm sorry that it happened to you. I'm sorry that it didn't kill Ethan and that it didn't kill Dylan or any of the other guys and that it hurt you instead. I know my sentiments don't take it back, but you seem pretty nice, and you didn't deserve any of this. You just got caught up with the wrong guy at the wrong time. It's happened to all of us, right? Most of us have carried the trauma of a bad guy before. It's just fucked up to have to carry it on your skin. I wonder if, with enough time, the people in the chain will forget the entire experience. Chalk it all up to a bad dream. Blame it on some bad weed.

It sounds like people get better with time. I mean you can't regrow a tooth or something, but with time hair comes back, skin heals, nails regrow. Soon people are like how they once were. I'm sure by now you've realized that. You're looking well. Your fingernails are almost all back. A good dentist and a good dermatologist will get you back on track. There are a few good ones closer to the city you might want to look into if you're interested. The sores have healed, yes, but you have scars. Your hair is growing back gradually, too. Getting the short cut was a smart move, it looks great on you. It makes your hair look fuller while the bald spots grow back.

Make sure to get yourself a decent therapist for the stuff that you can't grow back or get an implant for. They're sworn to secrecy and they can hook you up with the doctors that prescribe benzos. Although I don't have any suggestions for your sleeping problems. None of us can sleep anymore.

And no, I won't tell anyone who you are.

You weren't hard to find.

It is Jamie, right?

Carrie

ACKNOWLEDGMENTS

I wrote this book as a dare to myself.

Despite loving the art of writing, due to an overwhelmingly toxic cocktail of perfectionism and imposter syndrome, I spent the majority of my adult life actually . . . not writing much of anything. I was haunted by self limiting anxious thoughts, and every time I thought I had a story to tell, I pathetically withered away the moment things became hard.

And then one day, in late 2021, I got sick of my own excuses. I cleared out space in our spare room, bought myself a cheap laptop (the very same laptop I'm writing on now, albeit now pocked with peeling band stickers and notably missing the number "9"), and just began typing. I told myself I wasn't allowed to stop until I had something worth showing, dared myself to do something hard and allowed myself to be bad at it. At first, nothing came out. And then I kept going. And going. And gradually something started to form. It was difficult and slow moving and I wasn't very good at it, but eventually the words began to bleed out of me, and a cohesive story took shape, a story about revenge, feminine rage, isolation, and crippling grief.

I didn't think anything would ever come of it. I certainly didn't think anyone would ever read it. And I absolutely didn't think it'd ever be published.

Writing the thing is one of the most impossible tasks ever, but even that is only half the work. You've got to find someone who believes in you.

This book was only made possible because I found two people that do.

So I want to thank Max and Lori for seeing it and taking a chance on a nobody writer. It's hard to express how meaningful it's been for me to know someone out there not only feels that I have a story worth telling, but also a voice to tell it in. Thank you for Ghoulish Books existing at all, for that matter. It may be hard on some days to zoom out to the larger picture to see it, but giving independent writers a space to tell their stories is a treat to the craft and invaluable to those who've been allowed that space.

To Matthew Revert, thank you for being a saint through the process of cover design. I was relentless through revisions and fastidious, perhaps overly so, about tiny details and if you hated me, you certainly didn't show it.

Thank you to Jill Flaherty (I know it's Groff now but you'll never not be Miss Flaherty to me), for telling me that my 11th grade essay on cults was one of the best things you've ever read, but then pummeling my grade to a pulp because I didn't turn in the brainstorming, drafting, and editing steps. I wish I could say it pushed me to be a more systematic writer, but then in addition to being a disorganized mess, I'd be a liar as well. What it did do, however, was demonstrate to me that the raw ability to write was there, if only I could hone it. It also made for a really funny anecdote that I finally get to use.

Thank you to my mom for letting me kill you via vending machine in my 7th grade fiction, and only mentioning it every six months for the rest of our lives. Dad, I can't remember if I killed you or not, but thanks for being one of my angst fueled muses anyway.

Jessica and Jordan, thank you both for being my neverending sounding board and for the group chat/Wordle debriefer/band name generator/angel number scrapbook, which inadvertently birthed the title of this book. Not only are you both brilliant and hilarious and super talented women, but you're genius wordsmiths and honestly smarter than I'll ever be.

Endless gratitude and love to my husband, Tim. Not only can I say you support every one of my creative prospects in life, but you encourage me to act on them enthusiastically, relentlessly, and without fear. No matter what project I come up with, what shiny new interest I reveal has taken hold deep in my brain, your answer is always yes yes yes yes. You may not share the same love of the grim and macabre as I do, but you know the things that are important to me, and you lean in and tell me how we can make them happen.

I must also deeply credit my artistic muses: Paul Tremblay, Eric LaRocca, Stephen King, Gerard Way, Stephen Gammell, Geoff Rickly, Bo Burnham, Agustina Bazterrica, Nick Cutter. Thank you for making art for the weird kids.

And finally, I thank you, reader. Writers are nothing without readers, so neverending gratitude to you for taking a slice out of your very precious time in this world to spend it with me and my silly words.

ABOUT THE AUTHOR

Shannon Riley (she/her) is a writer and therapist who, as a teen, wrote gore starring her friends and family instead of doing math homework. Her short stories have been seen in the *Dark Blooms: Girls' Coming-of-Age Horrors* anthology, and in Ghoulish Tales. She lives with her husband and two daughters in a mediumish suburb just outside of Pittsburgh. If you like chatting about 2000s emo and post-hardcore music, you can find her on Twitter @shannon_said. *Pocketknife Kitty* is her first book.

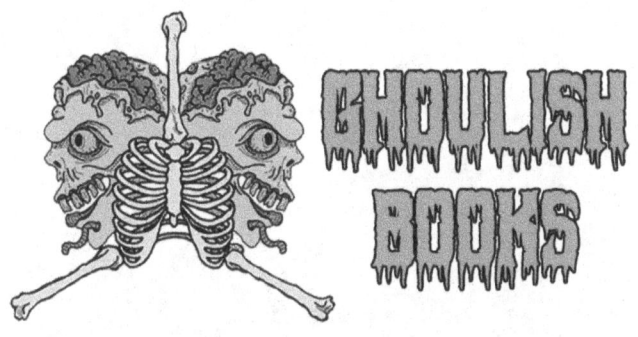

Patreon:
www.patreon.com/ghoulishbooks

Website:
www.Ghoulish.rip

Facebook:
www.facebook.com/GhoulishBooks

Twitter:
@GhoulishBooks

Instagram:
@GhoulishBookstore

Linktree:
linktr.ee/ghoulishbooks

www.ingramcontent.com/pod-product-compliance
Lightning Source LLC
Chambersburg PA
CBHW011436240626
47153CB00011B/3022